Marilyn P. Dorer

Dongola

*The University of Arkansas Press Award
for Arabic Literature in Translation, 1997*

Dongola

A NOVEL OF NUBIA

Written by Idris Ali

Translated from the Arabic
by Peter Theroux

THE UNIVERSITY OF ARKANSAS PRESS
Fayetteville 1998

Originally published by the General Egyptian Book Organization, in Arabic,
as *Dunqulah: Riwāyah Nūbīyah*

02 01 00 99 98   5 4 3 2 1

Designer: Rebecca Blakeney

⊖ The paper used in this publication meets the minimum requirements of
the American National Standard for Permanence of Paper for Printed
Library Materials Z39.48-1984.

Library of Congress Cataloging-in-Publication Data

Alī, Idrīs
    [Dunqulah. English]
    Dongola: a novel of Nubia/written by Idris Ali; translated
from the Arabic by Peter C. Theroux
        p.   cm.
    Originally published: Cairo: General Egyption Book Organization.
    ISBN 1-55728-531-4 (alk. paper). — ISBN 1-55728-532-2 (pbk. :
alk. paper)
    I. Theroux, Peter. II. Title.
PJ7812.I23D813   1998
892.7'36—dc21   98-3151
                                                                   CIP

Translator's Note:
Some additions, deletions, and small adjustments have been made to the
English text of *Dongola: A Novel of Nubia,* with the consent of the author.

To Dr. Yusri al-Azab
and to my friends and loved ones, the people of the north

These are all my pages; do not tear them up
This is my voice; do not silence it
This is I; do not curse me
For I have lived among you and eaten with you,
  loved your culture, and still do. I am merely
  conveying to you, with the sting of truth, some of
  my sorrows, and those of my people.

Idris Ali

Contents

PART ONE

Separated Man

ILLUMINATION:

[Caliph] Umar wanted to secure the southern borders of Egypt, as he had secured the western borders. And so he sent 'Uqbah ibn-Nafi' al-Fihri to Nubia, but the people there fought the Muslims fiercely. 'Uqbah quickly withdrew without having concluded a peace or a truce, as the Nubians shot their arrows, never missing. They aimed only with their eyes when they shot, so the Arabs called them "the bowmen of the glance." Umar's battalions remained skirmishing on the borders after 'Uqbah's retreat. In the caliphate of 'Uthman ibn-'Affan, Abdallah ibn-Sa'd ibn-Abi-Sarh made a truce with them, though one side fought the other, and they made an exchange. The Nubians gave the Muslims slaves, and the Muslims gave the Nubians food equal to the value of the slaves. The Nubians did not even think of crossing the borders into Egypt to engage the Muslim forces, but were content to repel their enemy from their own land, and to stay on guard against them.

Dr. Muhammad Husayn Haykal,
Al-Faruq Umar

DISGRACE:

The Arab tribes which established themselves in the region of Murais in the early centuries of Islam trafficked in slaves from Nubia, and they kidnapped some Nubians and sold them to merchants in Egypt. Also, the raids Egypt mounted against Christian Nubia yielded Nubians as captives, and the Arab tribes trafficked in them.

Al-Maqrizi recounts that when 'Abd-al-Rahman al-'Umari had conquered the Nubians in the place known as Bashanqir, between Barbar and Abi Hamad, "slaves were so plentiful with their owners, that when one of them had his hair cut, he gave the barber a slave."

Dr. Mahmud Muhammad al-Hariri,
Aswan in the Middle Ages

1

The regular broadcast was interrupted, and the radio announcer solemnly declared, "This is Cairo," then fell silent. Military music blared, heralding urgent news or some national or international catastrophe.

Awad Shalali grew tense and nervous. His trembling fingers failed to light his cigarette. He waited warily, with all his senses—with his whole being. The minutes grew longer, and then the voice sounded, announcing: "Citizens! The bulletin is as follows: Today the President arrived at Cairo Airport, and was received by"—there was a list of bureaucrats—"and masses of the people."

He smacked the radio with the palm of his hand and turned

it off, laughing at his own naiveté, at having thought the news had something to do with his comrades, even though, if they had wanted, they could have taken them by force, and secretly. Anxieties had plagued him for a week, committing him to total silence on what was allowed and what was forbidden. No one spoke or opened a window except to get fresh air. For a long time he was in fear of anyone who knocked or asked questions: the mailman, and the reporter who brought notifications and news bulletins, and the strange walls with ears. When the days passed and no trouble came, he finally believed in the general amnesty enacted by a republic-wide resolution, not spoiled by the counter-orders of slaves. The sweetness of freedom swept over him, blessing him after ten nervous years. His confidence returned. He opened the windows. He joked with his uncle's guests who helped him seal the baskets and pack his suitcases. They argued with him over the messy state of the apartment and the apartment itself. He combed his frizzy hair and said, "Anything I can do, Uncle?"

"Go downstairs. Take a walk and meet me at the station."

Farewell, apartment of memories. Jazuli went into his nephew's closed room before it was invaded by hands that took away and sold its contents. Everything was as it had been for years: the dust and cobwebs, the books, papers, and clothes. On the wall beside the first bed was a picture of his oldest son, Dahab Jazuli, in the uniform of an army lieutenant, and other photographs of a beautiful, anonymous northern girl, a famous male singer, and soccer players. Beside the other bed was a picture of Bahr Jazuli, his younger boy, a law student, beside pictures of Maxim Gorky, Tolstoy, Dostoyevsky, and Lenin. This was a house of sorrows. The oldest had died defending the borders of the north and had been swallowed by the sands of the Sinai. The youngest had been in prison, until they had murdered him, but claimed he had deserted. His wife went mad with grief over the loss of her two sons. Jazuli prepared to move back south with Awad; he transferred his bank deposits and sold some land he owned, and they would leave the capital together this afternoon.

"Go on, boy," his uncle encouraged him when he saw him hesitating.

The house was crowded with visitors, well-wishers, and hagglers. They offered belated condolences on his father's tragic death, and irritated him with their questions and advice—all "God has said" and "the Prophet said."

He was irritated by them, and their chatter, and this place. As he went down the stairs, he heard exclamations of *Allahu akbar* over the ruse of the aggressor, and he understood that the people were distracted from him by more important battles to liberate the countries from the ocean to the Gulf. This was the second day he had left his voluntary prison. Yesterday he had been afraid; he saw all these northerners as spies. He imagined his every step to be his last.

Today he greeted the world happily because this was the day he was saying goodbye. Final release. He was seized by a violent nostalgia for the places he loved, men he knew, memories. He set out on his excursion through the most beautiful streets of the heart of the north. As he wandered he was struck and astonished, not believing what he saw. These were not the people of Egypt, not with these scowling faces, pursed lips, cold smiles, and bad jokes. They bumped into one another and blasphemed and cursed one another. Surely this was the effect of the high prices or the war in Yemen or the pressure of the soldiers who occupied every street and post. People hurried to their homes, terrorized.

What had happened to this once-laughing city? It used to be lovely. They had called it "Mother of the World"; now she was eating her children. What rapaciousness. For a long time he had had an addict's love for Cairo and everything in it. He had eaten lupin seeds and *koshari*, Abu Zarifa's stewed fava beans, al-Hati's kebabs, and Haj Khalil's pastries. He had visited the bazaars of the Muski and stood for a long time at the historic wall of the Ezbekia. He had exchanged friendly smiles with the beautiful women sitting on the marble benches along the Corniche al-Nil. He had been part of it all. It was they who had turned on him and soiled his innocence. He had pulled away from them, crazed. Ten years! They blamed the leader of the country for what had happened to them. The judge himself had hesitated, faltered, and thought it over. Even so he sentenced him and Bahr Jazuli to ten years each. And when they had served their time, they were brought by truck to the detention camp. But what had happened to this city of light and gaiety? A shadow of militarism and fear had fallen over it. A spy tailed everyone who grumbled and came between every couple who quarreled. A third informant lay in wait for a slip of the tongue. The writers of reports were busy. *It has come to our attention . . . Our secret sources have observed . . . Surveillance of the subject has revealed that he . . .* If you forgot to applaud the leader's motorcade you disappeared. A thoughtless word was the downfall of both speaker and listener. Prisons multiplied, grew, and took new forms. There was no deliverance for offenders. Once he had been with them. He had demanded evacuation or certain death. He cursed the King and the English. He enthusiastically applauded the soldiers of the revolution. But these ten years had cut him off from them forever. He ran to look, and the spies around him and behind him and inside him upset and unnerved him and hampered his steps. Overpowering fears again seized him. He passed in front of the Café Riche, his comrades' meeting place. He looked in searchingly and retreated in disgust when he saw the traitorous comrade surrounded by dupes. The bastard. He passed the Stella Bar and the apartment of his friend the doctor, upstairs in the insurance building. He would have liked to have spent his last hours with him, but he was afraid.

He kept walking, to the Qasr al-Nil Bridge. The two lion statues were still there, without whiskers. Feminized lions. A city under siege. Who should he sit with? Where should he spend the time he had left? Stranger in a strange city. He suddenly felt an unendurable thirst. He went into the Casino al-Nil and ordered a beer and a double: "Shit!" The ratlike waiter chided him, "What's that supposed to mean? Everything's fine. Everything couldn't be better." They all said the opposite of what they really felt. He tossed back the double in one gulp and felt his insides ignite. This was terrible, adulterated liquor. Fraud. On the first of his visits to the north, he had been met at the gate of the railway station by a swindler who sold him a Russkov watch. He asked for a quarter liter of cheap Bulanaki brandy, specifying that the bottle be brought unopened—for he knew well their ability to infiltrate the smallest places: pregnant bellies, married peoples' bedchambers, and even solid matter, because they were geniuses at painting the air itself, at sealing sunshine in bottles. He had to get out before it was too late, to leave the north and get back to his family. They swindled one another and fought. It was their own business. The passengers from a strange abode sang; yes, exile, the key to his crisis with the thinking of the north. For those soldiers, they puffed themselves up and some of them behaved as tyrannically as pharoahs, finding no one but Ramses to boast of. They brought his colossal statue and set it up in the square in front of the railway station so that every passenger arriving and leaving could see him. He did not like this Ramses, or any other pharaoh, because they were invaders. He drank the cocktail with the beer and looked bewilderedly at the people sitting and passing by. They rarely protested or rose up. Those spread out among the customers were mostly government spies: the photographer, the flower sellers, the shoe blacks, and others. He was getting drunk and thought of playing with them and testing them. He called out loudly to catch their attention.

"You have one day left, you tyrant!"

A policeman on the bridge looked directly at him. The passengers cursed and drew close to the shore and anchored under the casino. The shoe shiner hurried toward him and crouched at his feet. Another waiter came with a new appetizer, wiped off the table twice, and spoke to him to draw him into a conversation.

"Anything I can do for you, sir?"

He looked him over to try and establish which service he worked for. He ignored him, and the waiter spoke up again.

"Where are you from, friend?"

He sipped at his glass and said to himself, "What do you care, fool?" He let him go on talking to himself.

"Sudanese?"

"I'm Leb—"

All three of them laughed.

"Anything you want, sir."

"There is something I want."

"Anything."

The shoe shiner interrupted them:

"There's nothing but injustice in the world."

Now he was between two spies, and had an opportunity to insult one or both of them. He started with the waiter, motioning him to bend down. He lowered his head to him, and whispered, with mock embarrassment, "I want a woman. Can I get one?" The waiter drew away angrily, which gave him a juvenile delight. The shoe black finished the job, saying, "You know, sir, this country of ours should be burned down." He said to himself: So what are you waiting for? He looked at the shoe black's box and noticed it was strangely clean and shiny. His caution returned when he remembered the Wahat detention camp, and he left the shoe black cursing and mocking, crooning some song. He watched the photographer approach him.

"Souvenir picture, sir?"

Liquor dragged men to ruin. He laughed and answered the photographer.

"On condition I can be naked, next to the statue."

And now here came the flower seller, hovering nearby. The people of the north—how wrong they were to think themselves clever, even though . . . He drank another glass and recalled his father's wife, Ruhia, the murderess from Bulaq; a sudden smothering depression overcame him. The bitch. Yesterday, he had gone to look for her, planning to strangle her, if only he had been able to ascertain that she had slipped his father poison once she had colonized him and bled him dry. His naïve father had imagined the civilization of the north to be just one white-skinned, succulent woman with heavy buttocks and exposed breasts. He had fallen prey to this beastliest of women, a professional manhunter. With her sweet tongue, shiny satin dresses, and elaborate lace, she used desire to chew him up and spit him out, to inspire lust with her lips. Her target was Shalali's father, who earned good money as a waiter at Shepheard's Hotel. She threw him food: her luscious body. She flirted with him, cooked him stuffed vegetables, washed his clothes, sang him songs that celebrated brown skin, and observed him beside the shared washbasin, through the light shaft. She left him no peace. He needed her madly, but she would not give herself to him outside of marriage. He pounced on her, forgetting his son and his son's mother. Father and son, each of them chose a different way of dealing with the civilization of the north: dying of love, or of thought. Cyanide. The memories brought him back to the beginning of his tribulation.

"What is your name?"

"Awad al-Shalali."

"Where are you from?"

"Halfway between north and south, in the area where Cambyses' army perished, where the army of the Muslims retreated in defeat, its soldiers' eyes gouged out. Now it's all become a water reservoir for the north."

"Please keep your answers short and to the point."

"But that's just a little of what you don't know about us."

"What is your religion?"

"I believe in justice."

"You mean you're a pagan?"

"That's what I believe in. Take it any way you want."

"How old are you?"

"I was born in the age of weakness."

"Is there anything else you have to say?"

"Yes. You have all put hatred in my heart."

Cruel men. They beat him as he had never been beaten before. They tortured him and did not let up until his intestines were nearly torn apart. Horror. He could hear the voice of Hushia, his mother: "My boy, don't go to the land of that snake." That was how she described Ruhia, her husband's second wife. Every summer, he came home missing her, since he had been a boy in school, and continued going back to the north: his holy place.

He spent a few months with Bahr Jazuli, went to the bookshops with him, to cultural symposiums, and the cafés frequented by writers. Then they met the group of the future, the doctor and the comrades. They dreamed of a better world, which turned out to be prison and detention.

He drank as much as he could, to make up for ten years of thirst. He lost his balance and looked up, seeking a god to bring order to this chaos. He stopped looking, in despair. He saw the people of the north without heads: Bahr Jazuli hanged, dangling from the neck of one of the lions; his father as a corpse floating on the surface of the river; Ruhia engaging in lewd acts with the vagrants of Bulaq; and the terrible man, the bogey of the left, roaming the city in search of new victims and organizations to dream up. He saw the whole north as corrupt, where only cowards and informers got any glory—death to decent men. Where was the balance? Where was God?

Not long ago, when Awad went to Bulaq and asked about

Ruhia, the neighbors pretended not to know her; they resented her behavior. They cursed her. When he left, he met his old village friend Othman al-Kanzi; he welcomed him and told him every single detail of the tragedy. He sat and listened, grumbling, almost on the point of vomiting from the disgusting smells coming out of the nearby toilet, the smears of bedbug blood on the walls, the stink of bad breath and bad teeth, and the butts of Cotarelli cigarettes and the shabby wrappers. One day he dreamed with his comrades of sanitary rooms for all the people, and of blowing up these tombs, when this Othman was a farmer with land and a fine house on the banks of the Nile in the now-submerged land of Nubia. His house and land were now deep in the river, the reservoir of the north. He had been expelled. His father, too, had been a farmer before emigrating to the north to work as a doorman; that was before he got the job at the Shepheard's. Once he visited him in front of one of the elegant buildings in Zamalek. He saw him bowing to people, old and young, always obeying the calls of the silly women who tormented him with trips between the market and the floors of the building, perhaps to buy a bag of salt or a bunch of watercress. At the time, he felt hatred and disgust, and more than ever deeply attached to his comrades' thinking. Equality. Justice. Othman al-Kanzi. Did he know the origin of his family name, the title Habbatallah Abu-al-Makarim? Kanz al-Dawla, "the treasure of the state," was one of the good-for-nothing Arabs who was sent in to conspire against the peace of the south so the Ayyubids could take advantage of it? One of his children had seized northern Nubia and named it Bilad al-Kunuz, the Land of Treasures. Raiders of every nation left their countries, coveting other people's land.

Bahr Jazuli embraced a fanatical view of the south and smuggled in an article which attacked the idea of expelling the people of Nubia, of Silsilah Mountain. They grabbed him then, and he never came back. Awad was loyal to Bahr and took up the burden of the returning to the era of the "bowmen of the glance," planning for a new Dongola and an independent, unified Nubia despite his comrades' opposition to his secessionist ambitions. But how could he realize the impossible dream after the battalions of al-Zahir Baybars had annihilated the knights of Nubia? Awad Shalali was drunk. He stood up, singing "To whom shall I go?" and marveling—how had just one man done all this? The remains of the pilgrims!

Othman al-Kanzi went on unearthing the life of the man who had died of love.

"When your father's money ran out, Ruhia left him and went looking for some other bank, some healthier dupe. I heard her with my own ears, boy, when she used her filthy tongue on him— 'Yes, brother, you're all that's left, you skillet bottom black, still trying to tell me what to do? Get out, then. Go home to your black woman. Is she sitting and waiting for you there with that ugly face of hers?' She insulted him and insulted us along with him. We advised him and told him what was behind her terrible behavior: 'Listen, Shalali, she's a low-class woman. Do yourself a favor and divorce her.' But he never saw beyond her ass. That was until he caught her himself, one day, when she was with some good-for-nothing boy at the Ali Baba Cinema. He brought her home—he was in a rage. He tied her up and cut her hair off and took off her gold bracelets. He took the hidden money and the deed, all of which he'd earned with the sweat of his brow, and then he kicked her out. The sneaky bitch hung around and cried outside the door, and said things that would melt a stone, things, my boy, that sweetened and flattered him and played with him. She reminded him of how it used to be, and swore by Imam Hussein's head that she was faithful, and wrongly accused, and always would be. She said she'd be his servant. The poor man believed her and took her in. We heard them making up and crying, then laughing like they were smoking hash. We cursed him and withdrew to our room, just amazed at this cuckold who had lost his dignity. At midnight we were woken up by his screams. We hurried to him and found him throwing up and having diarrhea. We took him to the Qasr al-Aini Hospital, but he died before dawn. We made an official statement and demanded an autopsy. But things went her way, and the bitch got out of it easily. This fucking city—money's everything.

"Tell me, Awad Shalali. Why did they put you in prison?"

"What did you hear?"

"Talk."

"Such as?"

"They say none of you believe in God and his Prophet."

How could he explain? Even simplifying the story would not make him understand. This stinking room, this pathetic life, and the peasant and day-worker soldiers who had tortured him. His old passion to explain and to persuade was dead, and the facts had revealed lies and illusions. Some of his comrades were just taking advantage; they did not believe what they were saying, and there were so many defeatists and cowards among them. He said goodbye to Othman and left. He saw Abu Talib Effendi on the street corner, his face buried in a newspaper to hide his identity. He approached him provocatively and said, "Greetings, Arabs." He hated the Arab expatriates like Kanz al-Dawla and the bandit al-Omari, and he hated the trashy Mamelukes like al-Zahir Baybars. He hated the pharoahs and Ruhia and the present ruler. Effendi was shaken, but stutteringly returned his greeting. He left him sweating and strolled through the alleys of Bulaq, following in the footsteps of Ruhia, asking about her of people he assumed to be her relatives. This was even though he knew she was nothing, a low-class slut. At this very moment she might be underneath some other jackass whose name she didn't even know. Black, white, Arab, barbarian—it was all the same to her. All she wanted was money and some brawny idiot. She was a whore—there was no doubt about that. He bought a newspaper and saw a picture of the leader with his pharaonic nose. He also saw a picture of the informer gracing the literature page. The bastard. Stinking alleys full of mud and mire from the filthy water dumped out from the balconies after baths at dawn. He walked through the neighborhoods of al-Qalayah, Darb Nasr, Sabtia, Sheikh Ali, outer and inner Adawia, and Turjuman. A vulgar boy cursed at him in the filthiest language: "A savage! Come here, come here. He came into paradise, they cut—" He watched a bloody battle between Upper Egyptian cudgels and city pocketknives. Before, they used to gather the Upper Egyptians together and make them go around the alleys, shouting, "Who are you voting for? Dalal Hussein. Hussein Dalal. Men who love worms die in and get eaten by worms." Then they say, in the days of the Revolutionary Council, "Gamal! Gamal!" They deployed them in front of the election committees to terrorize people. He saw a group of workmen in a hash den, smoking their pipe and listening to Umm Kalthum. They would certainly all get stoned and stagger home to their stinking rooms, to sleep with Bulaq women with plump buttocks and soft flesh made silky with depilatories. The women would get pregnant and give birth to children who would grow up and become expert at cheering on the winner, the oppressor, the king, the sultan, the president, thinking, like their ancestors, that their mother's husband was their uncle. How could this be, as strangers could not be uncles?

—

Awad Shalali still sat by the riverside. He ordered another bottle of beer and drank it. Tonight he was catching the train south, going home to his mother who had been waiting for him for ten years. He would break his ties to the north, leaving behind him the comrades who had announced the dissolution of their political party and making their peace with the ruler, the prisons, the fear, the murderers of Bahr Jazuli, Ruhia, the soft

men, the robotic army officers, the paper shufflers, the traitorous comrades, and the north—with all its good and bad. For a
moment he tried to think logically about it all. He thought perhaps his father might have died of alcohol poisoning, or after
unintentionally ingesting some of the depilatory paste Ruhia used
between her thighs, or he might have committed suicide because
of his impotence with her. And perhaps Bahr Jazuli had deserted;
perhaps he had not been beaten to death as he thought. Perhaps
his comrades had been planning some big move behind his back.
How could he know their plans when he had spent a summer
with them, and then only through letters and leaflets? And this
photographer—perhaps he really was what he appeared to be,
and not a spy for the intelligence or military, or the border intelligence, or the chief executive, or the military penal police, or
the bureau of investigation, or State Security, or the Qasr al-Nil
police station, or the special intelligence forces of this or that
Mameluke. God, how many secret agencies were there in this
northern country? And who were they all working against? It
was the destructive doubt that led him one day to heaven itself.
Anyone who had tasted the horrors of the military prison could
never imagine the existence of any other hell. And the paradise
that blessed the few on earth had to be seized by force. His
memory again brought him to the end; as was his habit, every
summer, he came after the end of the academic year, but this
time, to buy what he needed for his wedding, which had been
arranged. His mother had told him insistently: "My boy, let me
marry you off and celebrate, because I worry about you and
those Egyptian women." He had never thought of northern
women; Ruhia had put a barrier between him and them forever.
He went along with it, and when he met with his comrades, Bahr
Jazuli suggested inviting them to the wedding party. They were
excited, because he was the most active and enthusiastic of the
comrades; they were university professors, students, and workers. They paid the travel fees from their own pockets and bought

a wonderful gift, a golden key to Cairo. They all rode the eight
o'clock train proudly, chatted and laughed, and told cruel jokes
about Upper Egyptians and Nubians. One of them said, joking:

"I'm afraid they'll eat us down there."

"Are they still cannibals down there?" said the other, pretending to be surprised.

"Don't worry, we just don't like jackass meat," Bahr Jazuli
told them.

They laughed for a long time, then talked seriously about
how best to get the people of Nubia to rebel—they worshiped
their masters after only the deity himself—and how to recruit
new comrades to help Awad Shalali. They waited patiently when
the train stopped after al-Minya station and was shunted on to a
disused branch line. Then security men pounced on them. He
invited them to a southern wedding. They led him to a northern
massacre.

"The accused, Awad Shalali."

"I am here."

"Why did you visit Cairo every summer?"

"I loved it there."

"What is your relationship with these people?"

"They are the finest people in Egypt."

"Did you know of their intention to overthrow the
government?"

"How?"

"We ask the questions around here!"

"What am I supposed to say?"

"We have proof that you have traveled among the villages
of Nubia and even as far south as Halfa and Dongola."

"That is all my country."

"We have proof that you spread dangerous ideas among
the people."

"I was enlightening them."

"About what?"

"Justice."

"Who made you do it?"

"It was my duty."

"Sign here."

"I insist on reading the transcript of the interrogation. I'm not illiterate."

"We're the ones who taught you how to read, you son of a slave."

"I object. My mother is a free Nubian lady."

"You'd be better off just signing."

"I want to read it first."

"The government was wrong to give you people schools. If we had left you savages, you'd still be our waiters and doormen. Take this man away and teach him some manners."

———

He had finished the bottle of beer and sat looking around. The river brought calamities that fit the north. The spies swarmed around the customers, seeking prey. He was still the prisoner of the past. Yesterday, when he had failed to find Ruhia, he had gone to the Bulaq police station to lodge a complaint against her. He had found a crowd of people and a fight over the officer sitting motionlessly behind the ledger. The victim of a crime was standing there, being slapped repeatedly, while the criminal was seated comfortably because he was one of the elite of Bulaq. The officer spoke angrily when Awad Shalali worked his way through the crowd and approached him. "Yes, sir, it has been a black day since morning. What's the problem? . . . Pickpocketed? Got into a fight? . . . Someone must have sold you a bridge." Everyone laughed. He swallowed, and swallowed the insult, looking in amazement at the informers, soldiers, and witnesses sipping cool drinks at the criminal's expense and snatching his expensive cigarettes. Then they all agreed that the victim had knocked himself to the ground and made offensive remarks about religion and the government. The perpetrator said he had forfeited his rights, but God's right was impossible, and he demanded absolutely that they expurgate the transcript of the blasphemous words of this young vagrant. Awad Shalali's astonishment grew when he read the motto *The Police Serve the People*; he realized that if Ruhia came here, she would bring her own witnesses, and perhaps even accuse him of raping her. They might put him in prison. He changed his mind and said the first thing that came into his head.

"I have come to make a report about the missing Bahr Jazuli."

"Who might he be?"

"My cousin. My mother's sister's son."

"And where did this happen?"

"In Wahat Prison."

"What are you saying, mister?"

"I swear he is buried there."

"What does that have to do with us?"

"Aren't you the police that serve the—"

"Look, mister, everyone has his special area. Go to the Wahat police."

"Leave, you mean?"

"Go to the public prosecutor or the interior minister. Wait. What did you say? Wahat? You mean the detention camp? Oh. Goodbye."

He turned to leave, and heard the sergeant say to the corporal beside him, "This guy looks black, but he's a red."

Awad Shalali turned to him and spoke with violent anger.

"The blackest thing is the day your parents conceived you. And it's your monkey ass that's red."

The sergeant, soldiers, informers, the perpetrator, the victim, and even those who had nothing to do with them got up and surrounded Awad Shalali, trying to get at him. He shouted at them and threatened them, saying that he would kill anyone who touched him. He was out of his mind. There was a commotion and noise. It caught the attention of the head officer, who hurried in and said, "Attention!" They all stood at attention, like the pickets of a fence, and saluted. These really were frightened people—unabashedly frightened.

"Do you like what he said, sir?" asked the sergeant, as if to bait his superior. "Are we supposed to do nothing when he insults the government?"

"Are you the government?" snapped Awad.

"We should arrest him, sir," said one hostile informer.

"I never thought I'd see this," said the criminal. "My grandfather had ten of these people, apart from the ones he gave their freedom to please God. I never thought I'd see the day they would turn on their masters."

"Which grandfather do you mean?" Awad Shalali taunted. "The one who used to lick the boots of the Mamelukes? Or the one who pimped women for Napoleon's soldiers?"

"Please!" said the corporal in a tone of warning.

"He has to be taught a lesson, sir," said the sergeant.

"That is all," said the corporal firmly.

"A slap or two would teach him," raged the criminal. "But no, let him go have a beer. Listen, leave him to me. My boys are outside—they'll take care of him. Mamelukes, he says!"

"I said, that's enough," said the corporal. "You may leave, sir."

"I won't be satisfied until that criminal is under arrest, and you hang Ruhia, and you catch the people who killed Bahr Jazuli."

Then he told them goodbye and went away, and they burst out laughing behind him. The sergeant sniffed, "What did we do to deserve that?" and the informer voiced his agreement. Awad Shalali strode along briskly, filled with rage that tore him to pieces inside, rage that the Bulaqi man was so proud that his grandfather had owned slaves. Slaves owning slaves! He stopped and stood in Gala' Street, looking around as people ran by, lined up, and applauded a passing motorcade, chanting that they would give their lives and blood for the leader. They had said the same of every leader before. He had liked this man when he had said, "Hold your heads high—the days of slavery are over." He hated him when he threw them into prison, and his hatred still endured. He stood amazed at this insane enthusiasm, his hands thrust into his pockets. The man beside him nudged him, frightened: "Clap, you stupid black; are you looking for trouble?" But he left before the celebration reached its climax and went to the Nubian café in Abdine to look for some old friends. He sat at a distance, and they greeted him in gestures. They were afraid. The Nubian band, led by Ali Kuban, was singing in praise of the Aswan Dam and the revolution. The presidents of charitable societies had sent cables of support: "Proceed, with God's blessing. We are behind you." They were not the descendants of the bowmen of the glance. They had lost Nubia, their past, and their present. He cursed them all and wandered out.

~

He ordered a glass of beer and watched the crowds crossing the bridge, waving red and white flags. Had war broken out? Between who and whom? One of the marchers shouted excitedly:

"Ahli's number one!"

"Zamalek's the greatest," someone responded.

A third man danced:

"Ahli's number one! Ahli's number one!"

He felt dizzy as he tried to establish the location, on the map of the world, of the two countries at war. But an angry voice broke in on his effort to remember, because a stressed man's nerves could not endure this kind of stupidity. The voice shouted, "These are the most bizarre people on earth! What Ahli? What Zamalek? We don't have enough to eat, and we live under the protection of the international police!"

The photographer ignored his anger and took a rare documentary photo. The shoe black approached from the hot area. The flower seller hurried away. Two respectable men entered, calmly escorting the angry man. A few people got up and left. Lovers fell silent. Awad Shalali stayed where he was, watching the passersby, so drunk that he thought they were soldiers marching south, to destroy the south and return with booty and plunder, and thousands of what they called slaves, though they were actually citizens of that country. Which expedition was this? The most destructive had been the Pharaoh Snefru, though he was followed by butchers. The most repulsive were Shams al-Dawla, Turan-Shah, and the bloodiest of all, al-Zahir Baybars, still a deity in the north. He cursed them all, including the wanton Nubian King Shakandah, the traitor. He cursed Kanz al-Dawla and Sir William Wilcox, chief of the treasury, the pashas, the sultans, Muhammad Ali Pasha, and all the ministers of irrigation who had ever lived and those still to come, and anyone who had placed a single stone in the first and second dams. He cursed the river that had surrendered to the dam, and he cursed the whole world, which had helped to save the temples, while leaving the people to their fate. His blood boiled. He grew tense. He rose from his seat and shouted in his loudest voice, "You sons of whores!" He heard a voice answering him from far away— "Who are you swearing at, you asshole?" Someone else said, "Leave him alone—he's just a stupid Zamalek supporter. All the servants are for Zamalek."

The owner of the bar came over with the waiters and demanded he pay. They overcharged him and then made him leave. At the door he was met by the informer, in galabia and overcoat, who led him to a dark corner near the Revolutionary

Command Council building, searched him, took the change in his pockets, a pack of cigarettes, and his lighter, then let him go. He walked along the Corniche, staggering, until he saw a gate and stairs that led down to the river. He descended with difficulty, then pushed two fingers down his throat and vomited, ridding his stomach of the remains of liquor and bad food. He washed his face in the river water. He roused himself, dunked his head in the water, and felt totally recovered, then mounted the stairs. He heard the roar of the crowd after the early goal that landed in the Ahli net and felt sure that war must have broken out. He kept going and found himself in the middle of the crowd. Tahrir Square. He saw things with a clarity that lifted fog around simple truths: those marching figures were not invading soldiers, but weary northerners going home after a hard day, and they were not hostile or hateful. They were not all the murderers of Bahr Jazuli. The murderers were a terrible minority who made no distinction between northerners and southerners, infidels and believers, Muslims and Copts. Nor had they any hand in the destruction of the south or the enslavement of its valiant people. Ruhia may have been a corrupt woman and a murderer, but she represented a minority of northern women. The trouble was that his father had made a poor choice. Some of the northern women were decent, cultured, and politically enlightened. If he met even the most beautiful of them, they would never refuse him because of his color, because Aba-al-Misk Kafur al-Ikhshidi, a Nubian slave, had once sat on the throne of Egypt. Yes, Cairo was beautiful, and its people were full of goodness and tolerance. Those who had invaded the south and laid it waste had done that with older cultures and more powerful nations. Those who had times ruled by brute force and stupidity. What had happened to him was just a passing thing, and he would survive it. He threw off his gloom and winked at a young girl who gave him a smile that delighted him. He joked with a man peddling phony watches and gave some money to a beggar. He helped a blind man cross the street. He called the doctor, grateful and friendly, for he had not forgotten that this man had taught him two valuable languages in prison. He bought the evening newspaper and hurried to the station with a heart brimming with restored love. The train was about to pull out, and he jumped on board and searched through the cars for his uncle.

2

The slow train to the south, and its strange third class. The mess. The crowds. Chaos. An abyss of random objects. The passengers were Upper Egyptians, Nubians, and Sudanese. Robes and turbans. Simple people. Army soldiers occupying the overhead luggage racks, their boots dangling over the riders' heads, ready to be removed to administer a beating. Awad refused to ride in first class because of that memory, and his uncle supported him in that because he preferred socializing with his relatives to the prison of a sleeping car. But this train was unbearable, and he had a blinding headache and a pain in his ulcerous stomach. For hours he had made peace with the world and himself and his mother country, but was once again sinking into a depression. The wooden seat made him sore, and the dust blowing through the broken windows was suffocating him. The noise and the fights that broke out over nothing, or their backward ideas: cudgels raised, with a head almost smashed because one of them had cursed the other and called him a jerk when he is a water carrier in Upper Egypt. Here were boors and irregular troops, Ansar and Jaafaris, honorable sherifs, Kanzis, Nubians, Halab and Noor, gypsies and Basharis and Ababidis, Arab descendants of the Prophet and nomadic Arabs, peasants and Copts and Muslims, descendants of the Prophet's disciples, and those who claimed to be. Origin and boasting and judgment. Once he had dreamed of a train with all the classes united, in a country in which no one was fanatical about color or religion, but about justice. It was for such principles they had thought, theorized, and gone to prison. He had dreamed of food distributed equally— why were the people of the capital city blessed with plenty, while others died of illness and starved? After the successive elevations leading up to the reservoir at Aswan, he came face to face with his people, in their terrible predicament—culturally and existentially—ever since losing their land. Drought and famine. It was his bad luck to have been born in the time of famine. He remembered his miserable childhood with anguish, spending nights with an empty stomach when they had not succeeded in finding wood for cooking. He ate a disgusting thick paste called *ambudays*, made of brackish water, oil, salt, and black bread. He ate rotten pickled fish called *tarkeen*, left uneaten even by the dogs; he ate powdered salt and beanstalk leaves, called *kashr najij*. He ate sparrows, locusts, cranes, foxes, and dry bread. Fish was plentiful, but oil to fry it in was scarce. For sweets, they ate sesame seed meal with molasses when they could find any, which was rare. Meat and fowl were for religious feasts and the homecoming of their exiles and expatriates, for guests, and for funerals. He attended the compulsory school barefoot, in the one long shirt he wore in summer and winter; his lunch sack held two dates or an egg. On free days, he ate a pancake of rare wheat flour, called *tajin-kul*. The road to the cemetery was often traveled, because the nearest medical clinic was a day away by boat—two days by donkeyback or walking, through pathless mountains where fierce animals lurked. The village's resident doctor was an ignorant barber, and his only instruments were a straight shaving razor used for circumcisions and bloodletting, near ulcerated eyes; cupping glasses; nails for the back of the neck and heads; string for pulling out molars; he had herbs that ruined peoples' stomachs and prayers and amulets. Once, Awad got a fever and was treated by having the back of his neck and his head scarred with a hot nail. His body was

anointed with Nile mud full of bilharzia parasites. Only chance
kept him from death, though epidemics killed many of his friends:
malaria, cholera, yellow fever, and tuberculosis, to say nothing
of scorpion stings and snake bites. It was a forgotten land, which
the world had erased from its map, to serve as a reservoir for its
water. No king, sultan, or pasha had ever visited here. The only
president who felt affectionately toward them was assassinated.
Awad's naïve people imagined that their troubles resulted from
God's anger with them. But why would the deity be angry at
people who prayed and worshiped him, if that was the price of
pleasing him? When he was young and inexperienced, he imagined the whole world was just like this—until he visited the
North. He was thunderstruck. He was amazed. He was sure this
was the paradise the sheikh at the mosque talked about in his
sermons: all kinds of fruits heaped up on handcarts, all kinds of
meat hanging in front of butcher shops, clean white bread, pure
water, and electricity. People wore ironed clothes; their skin was
fair and they had rosy cheeks and were hardly ever barefoot.
Was this the same Egypt as his village, hanging perilously onto
a mountain, swimming invisibly in darkness, without a single
green leaf all the winter long? He later learned that all the bounty
of the North came from constant irrigation provided by the water
held in reserve above the land of Nubia. He grew angry and
hateful, and a never-ending sorrow entered his heart. This was
why, when he grew up and began reading, he so liked the ideas
of Bahr Jazuli and his comrades. From that day onward he hated
the preachers in the mosques who held out the image of that
imaginary paradise before the people. He hated his grandfather
and all the old men, because they had given in to the tyranny of
the North. He hated his father for entangling himself in the web
of the despicable Ruhia. He hated his grandmother who had filled
his head with the fairy tale of the jar of treasure. He hated the way
they numbed their pain with superstition and the pronouncments
of holy men, preachers, the Night of Power, accepting fate, and
people who made degrees. He hated fate and destiny and prayer,

the Islamic alms tax, the bank, the funeral train, public aid, and beggary. He hated more things than he could count.

No power could restore love to him before proclaiming the banner of equality. The night was long, and he still had a headache; the train was slow and broken now, almost a ruin. His uncle, who looked after him and his mother when they asked for help, smoked voraciously, and his sad, grave eyes stared intently at nothing. He was one of the mysteries of Cairo because of his work as a cook for the British ambassador and almost made it into the society of masters with his eldest son's graduation as an officer, while the younger was on the threshold of becoming a lawyer or parliamentarian. And now he was returning with loss and worry; his sadness was for the youngest, Bahr Jazuli. He wiped two tears away and asked in a grieving tone:

"Why did they kill him?"

"He was a man."

"Tell me about him."

"He loved you, Uncle."

"Tell me about him."

The day they arrested him he was Egyptian, but he died a Nubian. His extreme secessionist ideas had germinated in his prison cells and bloomed fully under the whiplash and daily insults. He was enlightened and knew all Nubian's willfully obliterated history. When his treatment grew worse, he led a hunger strike demanding improved conditions. An arrogant young officer antagonized him and helped, with his vicious behavior, to widen the gap. He insulted him in front of everyone with unnecessary cruelty.

"Are you the only one left, you son of a dish licker?"

His rage, and the harshness of the insult, pushed Bahr Jazuli to answer recklessly.

"That's right, I'm a son of a dish licker. But people who lick give honor to the dishes. Your dogs are cleaner than you are."

"Your heart is as black as your face."

"My blackness is a fact—I know where it comes from!

Not you—I think you'd better ask your grandmother where those blue eyes of yours came from."

If he told his uncle the details of what happened that day, he would have died of apoplexy. It was a day of bloody revenge he believed no creature had experienced before Bahr Jazuli. They took turns beating him with shoes and then punching him. He was left out in the blazing July sun to grow even blacker— "Even more authentic," they joked.

His uncle slept contentedly. The wretched train passed through the wretched country inhabited by the people of the inner and outer regions of Upper Egypt. The country road intermittently ran parallel to the train tracks. This was the road used for invasions when they headed south in search of ostrich feathers, musk, crocodile skins, livestock, and the gold they snatched from the arms and necks of women. But the true and real aim of the campaigns was always to take prisoners. They exported them for sale and as gifts to the vast Islamic state because they loved the strong slaves of Nubia. Perhaps they used them to build citadels and fortresses and sent them to their deaths in hopeless wars.

The villages flashed by, one after the other, and his worry mounted: Silsilah Mountain, then the resettlement camps of the land of Nubia, tin houses without a trace of beauty, with concrete roofs that reflected the heat; slender women with ebony faces, waiting for men who were scattered around the globe looking for a livelihood; and no one waited more impatiently than his mother. She trilled with joy and celebrated by throwing dates and popcorn over everyone's heads. They had a grand party and paraded him through town, as they always did for someone whose homecoming they had hardly dared hope for. They slaughtered a sheep and cooked it, splashing its blood on walls and doorways. The trills of joy brought unnumbered crowds from the neighboring villages of Alaqi, Kalabshah, Qurtah, and Maria. In old times, they had been divided between Egypt and Sudan like spoils of war. Now it was a monstrous homeland. The people of the north overcame crises by telling jokes; here, they gave parties. His mother danced, and danced beautifully, despite her age and her pains. The men lined up in two opposite rows, clapping and singing. Those who loved the voice of Abdu Shindi, the warbling vocalist of the Kanz, spread out in search of him, until they found him getting drunk near the railroad tracks. They dragged and pushed him to the dance floor despite his resistance. No one knew what had come over him since they had been displaced to this land. In the past, he was the one who had gone out searching for parties, to liven them up. His deep voice rose, affected by the Kanzi song of farewell for which he was famous. He improvised and grew happier, then extemporized a folk song about Nubia, which was now under water, with its palm trees, shadows, and small villages. Now boats and ships, floodwaters and fish, temples, mountains, crocodiles, and the tombs of the dead and of virgins. The men sat down and let him have the space, with a man beating a tambourine. His wounded voice rose to float beyond the boundaries of the village and attracted more listeners. Then his voice sank to a whisper like a sob. The children, elderly, and the ill left their houses and shuffled in their hundreds to throng the wide clearing between Qirshah and Alaqi. They were confused, not knowing whether they had come upon a wedding or a crowd of mourners. This was something they had never seen before. From among the assembly of women, sobbing was heard from a woman who had been forced to leave her village, for whom the songs brought to life memories she had tried to forget. What caused the explosion, which revealed the truth of their condition, was the singer Abdu Shindi himself, as he repeated the name of the river over and over, and linked it with treason. Then he collapsed to the ground and threw a handful of dirt on his head, and sang, in a soft, sad voice:

My land, my homeland, my abode,
land of my fathers, my palm trees, O Nubia
You are one, you are one, you are one.

The tearful voices behind him repeated the last verse with intermittent wails. An officer from the Kalabshah police station arrived, to spy out what was behind the gathering and this mass weeping. The more prudent people tried to intervene to stop the flood of tears that flowed without any direct, obvious cause. An ordinary celebration for the return of one of the absent had turned suddenly into a ceremony of nationalist mourning. Jazuli was affected by the sad situation and went with his emotions to the sands of the Sinai and Wahat; he remembered his two boys and burst into tears and began to engage in the funeral rites. He unwrapped his turban and wrapped it around his waist, and leaned on his stick and moved around the seated throng several times.

"Eternal God, my sons . . ."

The men followed him, all the men, even those who had ignored his story, and stayed behind him, repeating the words "Only God is eternal." Hushia al-Nur, the boys' aunt, and the mother of Awad Shalali, released one of her extended screams: *Biyu, biyu, biyu!* She jumped from among the women, tearing at her hair and rubbing dirt on her face, and crawled along the ground: *Ahi! Ahi! Ahi! Ahi! Ahi!* The women followed her, or most of them did, lined up behind Hushia al-Nur, holding their hands aloft in the air as they had done in days gone by. The men could do nothing to quiet them and let them take over the space. It seemed to be a belated celebration of nationalist mourning to grieve over drowned Nubia.

3

After the mourning ceremony the preceding day, Abdu Shindi became the talk of the villages of Nubia. His sad song had spread among old and young; they all sang it and wept with sorrow, the women sitting and waiting, remembering, as their eyes teared up, and the words brought back the men's memories of the streams and roots, and they too were overcome with despair and homesickness. Abdu Shindi had succeeded, unintentionally, in disturbing their spirits and stirring up their emotions. Awad Shalali tried laboriously to be philosophical about the meaning of what had happened, but the sorrows, tears, and songs would never restore the land that had been drowned, the identity obliterated, or the unhurried saviors—because they were here, not there. Nothing was left. Shindi would keep on singing, and turning weddings into funerals, but in vain. Here trains were always screeching to deliver an expatriate and to take away dozens of emigrants fleeing unemployment and despair.

Depressed at this repulsive place, Awad Shalali sat with his uncle on the bench to receive the people welcoming him home. A question bewildered him: How had they submitted to this reality and grown accustomed to it? His mother said that his former bride-to-be had married after too long a wait and borne two sons. It was up to him to repair the house and to choose the bride he wanted: "You just think about it, and I'll marry you to the best girl in Qirshah." His uncle encouraged him: "And I'll give you all the money you want!" At this moment he was not thinking about the women of Qirshah or of anywhere else. His mind was filled with the sad song. *My land . . . my palm trees . . . land of my fathers . . .* The watchman, Abbas Tawfiq, came up to him, affecting urgency:

"The officer at the station told me to bring you to him, sir."

"Did he give you handcuffs?"

"There's no problem, Abbas," said his uncle, sounding upset. "But what does the government want with us?"

Hushia al-Nur came out with a pitcher of tea and heard part of the conversation. She struck her hand against her chest and cried out, "*Hil-wa! Hil-wa!* What's wrong, Abbas?"

"Your son was fighting the government, Hushia!"

"Not exactly, Mother," Awad interrupted. He turned to Abbas to correct him. "We opposed, Abbas. We did not fight."

Hushia put down the pitcher of tea, frightened.

"The government?"

"I heard them saying at the station that you were inciting the people yesterday," explained Abbas Tawfiq.

"Me?"

"Everyone is tired, Abbas, all of us, and you, too," sighed his uncle.

Then he raised his hands and recited the *Fatiha* for the souls of his two sons. He wept, and all those sitting with him wept, and so did the people who were passing by. The younger son was dear to him. The northerners were devils. They had dragged him away with them to perish. Jazula collapsed, trying to stand and say mourning prayers, like yesterday. They held him and helped him to sit down again.

"Pray, Jazuli."

"Only God is eternal."

"All of us will die."

"God will punish oppressors."

Hushia al-Nur had not stopped crying. She had waited ten years, and she had no strength left. For her, as for all the people of Nubia, the government was an indomitable power. All of them were defenseless before this unarmed functionary. So, what was her son thinking? Would he not say he was sorry?

"Take pity on my old age, Awad," she begged him.

"Don't worry, Mother."

"So there's nothing wrong?"

"Just a little bureaucracy."

She did not look convinced. She ran along behind him, bareheaded and barefoot, wailing. They held her back by force. Awad Shalali entered the police station with his uncle, confident of his position, but the officer received him gruffly.

"You're Awad Shalali?"

Then, in a tense tone to his subordinates: "A car, and two informers, *now*."

4

What did they want from him? It was an unanswerable question which occupied him the whole time it took them to get from Kalabshah to the Directorate of Security in Aswan. He did not remember doing anything that had harmed security in a place where the security was never disturbed at all. He'd had absolutely no contact with his old comrades. Had they gone back on their decision to grant him a pardon? Had there been troubles in the north? Were they re-arresting people as a preemptive measure? He was not afraid. Nothing would happen to him—nothing worse than had already happened, anyway. But he pitied his mother and uncle. They pushed him into the presence of a secretarial officer, to provide the documentation that would be presented to the more senior official. It seemed they would not leave him in the state of these stupid people, even though he had left the field and had chosen exile in the south. He felt torment; his blood began to boil. He felt like the mutineer, Satan. The officer asked him the usual numbing questions:

"Your name in full?"

They were going to clash. He answered with a challenge in his voice.

"You want my real name?"

"Of course."

"Then write this down. My historical name is Taharqah. My homeland is the land of Nubia, which has been consumed by the pages of history. We were, but you made us not be. I have come to you to bring a lawsuit against the builders of the dam and the reservoir, and to seek my old borders, from Aswan to old Dongola, to establish a provisional government. I have decided upon the color of our flag. It will be black, with the pupil of an eye in the middle, and arrows. We have no objection to union with the north, and we will put that on the table for negotiation. Write, officer. Why did you stop writing?"

The officer had indeed stopped writing and was staring at him in surprise and unease. He exchanged looks of amazement with the standing officer and the informant with him and with the intelligence officer who had been pacing the office irritably.

"What kind of nonsense is this?" the seated officer asked angrily.

"You hate the truth."

"What truth?"

The standing officer intervened. He opened the file of Awad Shalali and studied it closely. Then he moved closer to Awad and sniffed his mouth. He could not find a medical report in his file that explained this delirium, nor was there any smell of liquor to justify what he had just heard. A lawsuit against the builders of the dam? Good God, against whom? This was something far beyond madness. He decided not to believe his ears, and asked:

"What did you say, my brother?"

"I said just what you heard, sir."

"Please explain it to me."

"I wasn't speaking Nubian, I was speaking Arabic."

"That was not Arabic, boy."

"So what was it?"

"The language of lunatics, fools, and clowns. We are here in a government office, and you're talking like you're in a bar or a drug den. I am going to ask you the same question myself. What is your name?"

"Don't waste your time, sir. I'm not going to say anything different."

"Just what is your story?"

"My story?"

"What is wrong with you?"

"It is the history of—"

"Good God, what have they done to you?"

"They killed Bahr Jazuli and stole ten years of my life."

"Fine. Fine. Have a seat and get ready to meet our boss, the director. You're a lot of work, for sure."

He had been a lot of work ever since he started reading history. He had always demanded justice and equality. Now his quest was harsh and arduous, provocative and destructive, extracting the part from the whole, identity, separation. He drew and planned out the coming arena of battle in his head. He counted the armies of the Kanz, the Fadja, the Mahas, and the Danakils. He went back and forth, east and west, between the valleys and the mountains. Reporters would go from scene to scene, now describing it all as a revolution of the descendants of the Mahdi Revolt—which the British called the revolution of the Dervishes—now as a new Revolt of the Zanj. He was determined that peace would be concluded on top of the High Dam. The revolution might fail, and then their severed heads would hang from the telegraph poles the whole length of the Upper Egyptian highway. A headache. A headache. They presented him to the official with the file. Another idiot like the others he had met in the wars and at Wahat. The peacocks retreated at the sight of the chair, which tottered backward.

"Listen, boy," he said threateningly. "Let me tell you the truth. I don't like communists, even if the government did make peace with you. My opinion always was that you should be executed, because you are apostates, and Islam allows us to kill you. I could wipe you out of existence if you did anything foolish. I have reports that prove you are a secessionist and a troublemaker, and that is a much worse charge than the first one because you are endangering the peace of this country. The best thing for you is to cooperate with me. Tell me the truth about your plans and ideas."

"The truth is, sir—"

"That's better."

"Give us back our old homeland."

"This is high politics!"

"Give us land fit for planting."

"And that is in the plan—"

"Build us factories."

"We will try—"

"Pay us compensation equal to what we lost."

"What more do you want?"

"Aren't we worth just as much as temples and statues?"

"My boy, these are things decided by the president of this country. It looks to me like you need some discipline."

"That's already been taken care of."

"What exactly do you want?"

"My people are tired of—"

"Talk about yourself."

"They are mute. The invaders have cut their tongues out."

"Be quiet."

"Has my master ordered me—"

"If you want to go back to your old country, we'll send you back immediately. But alone. Men, get a boat ready! And take this lunatic and drop him off in the farthest village in old Nubia, among the mad dogs and the beasts."

A sudden pang of alarm shot through Awad Shalali after the officer left the room to carry out this order. He pictured himself isolated and alone, being devoured by wolves. That would be a dramatic end, worse than Wahat, or being lashed to death. This idiot peacock could make it happen. Awad spoke up, trying to mask the quaver in his voice with sarcasm.

"Are you joking, sir?"

"The government never jokes, boy."

"Is that legal?"

"We are the law, you lucky man. Do you think I'd risk my position and my future for a cockroach like you? No, boy. Guess again."

Their conversation ended for a moment. What kind of a

conversation was it? A police general. A powerful man. The emblem of the crossed staff and sword on his shoulder meant something. They looked like scissors: a weapon. Had they killed Bahr Jazuli easily? He would welcome death, but not before he could act. He was awakened from his daydream by the voice of his conqueror.

"What do you think now? With one movement of my hand I can send out the bulletin that you're at large."

"Whatever you say."

"You've seen the light. I think we understand one another better now."

"Understand what?"

"Listen, my boy. We have no old feud between us. This is the first time I've ever dealt with you even though your name is on the blacklist. I could have had you expelled from the whole of Aswan the moment you arrived. I do not care about your red past. What bothers me is your black present. I heard about you from the mayor of your town. For your information, all the mayors and sheikhs and officials of Nubia are my friends. When I was young, you see, I worked in the police stations in al-Dur. I liked the people of Nubia, and they liked me. I'm a witness to their honesty, piety, and high morals. I do not know where you came from. If it weren't for my previous experience with your people, I would have turned you over to the security bureau and that would have been the end of you. I am asking you to cooperate with us, and you won't be sorry. We'll get you your job back, or any other job of your choosing. What do you say?"

"But why?"

"The reports say you were behind that mourning festival yesterday."

"Sir—"

"That's all. We're through here."

"What is your command, sir?" asked the other officer breathlessly.

"We have forgiven him again, on my own responsibility."

"You are a very lucky man, sir. Thank the officer."

When Abdu Shindi had sung his sad lament, and everyone's eyes teared up and their hearts bled, had he, Awad, been the instigator? When the people of the village gathered and held their ceremony, had Awad been their host? Awad felt his ulcers contract. He crossed the Aswan Corniche like a lost wanderer. This city always provoked him. It had a suspect role in its ties to the south; this was the bridgehead for all invaders, and all the Rabi'a tribesmen had come through here. They called it the Gate of the Nile and had made up for its role and built the reservoir and the dam far from it. He felt a violent nostalgia for the sight of Nubia before its final immersion. On the following day, the spies double-crossed them and started operating a boat, with a Nubian pilot, between the dam and Abu Simbel to carry UNESCO experts. They saw desolate villages on both banks, with all the doors torn off. When they returned, the Nubian pilot asked their leave and approached the target, the homeland of Awad Shalali, the village of Qirshah, facing Jurf Hussein and Maria. A Kanzi village had been relocated three times, as the reservoir rose, and then stayed there, on top of the mountain, until it was gradually submerged by the waters of the dam. This was the home of his childhood and memories. Here he had played and swum and made houses and dolls from the alluvial mud of the Nile. He chased the flocks of cranes that had flown from the lands of snow and ice. Once he had caught a lame bird and found an iron band on its leg, on which something was written in a language unknown to him. Awad brought the bird to Milayji Effendi, the Islamic schoolmaster at Qirshah, thinking it was either a bird from paradise or a demon. The schoolmaster said that this was a message from a society that looked after birds and wanted to know where the birds migrated. Milayji Effendi liked Awad immensely and had a greater influence on him than on the rest of the children. He sent him to the village to buy eggs and chickens. Milayji learned the dialect of Nubia from Awad, and one time asked about the meaning of *hanwa dol,* and Awad explained to him that it meant "the big jackass." Milayji laughed, and then got angry, and vowed to fire the school janitor or to break his head, because the janitor had described him that way.

Awad trusted Milayji and loved him, and visited him after he had grown up and gone on to the elementary school in al-Dikkah then to the teachers in Qurtah. There he found different kinds of books and read some of them, like *Robinson Crusoe* and *Creatures That Were Men* and collections of poetry of which he did not understand much. Once he read a book, which, to the best of his recollection, was called *The Roads of Hunger*, about a people who were going hungry, and so ate cats, dogs, donkeys, and even corpses. Awad went back to Milayji in fright to try and find out the truth of the matter, and Milayji said, "Yes, and this happened in Egypt, too, and it is written in the history of al-Jabarti." Awad's mother warned him against Milayji Effendi and tried to frighten Awad away from him because he was from Cairo, and a bachelor, and it was not right for young children to mix with foreign adults. Whenever he came home from Milayji's, she asked him what he had heard from him, and many, many other questions. But he never stopped visiting him, secretly or openly, though the men of the town were openly hostile to the man and wrote complaints and petitions against him until he was forced to leave. They said he did not pray, or fast in Ramadan, and taught the children that Shaykh Abd al-Rahim could not work miracles, and that the five tombs in the western desert were ordinary men who could not provide any cure or relief. This was why they said he was an infidel even though his religion was Islam. Awad had only good memories of Milayji Effendi, for it was he who had planted the seeds of learning in his head. He had searched for him for a long time during his stay in Cairo, but in vain. But he saw him once when he was being transported to the Wahat detention camp, and though he asked most of the prisoners about him, they never met again face to face.

He boarded the boat slowly at the inlet of Uliyat, stricken by memories, including the sounds of the ancient small villages: Juhurab, Danjarab, Shadnab, Harazah, Kilwa Dol, Ombo Kol, Hamaymtar, Naj al-Arab, Alyab, Jawharah, Qirshah, and Bayt Amudiyatha. Arabic, Pharaonic, and Nubian names, some of them meaningless. Some houses hugged the river, and others were closer to the mountains. In summer, when the river dropped and the land was visible, he went down with his mother to mow the couch grass and plant seeds. They sowed, but only rarely reaped. The north had glory and leisure; the south, death and floods. How many times had they been ruined by a flood coming out of season? Those days could never be forgotten, he said to the pilot. They drew nearer, approaching the end of the inlet by the bridge that connected two hamlets. He got out and went up, climbing a hill. One of the experts took a photo of him. When another generation had passed, archaeologists and others would come and write lies. He climbed a little higher, then retreated impatiently. The mad dogs ran behind him, following him. He threw himself into the river and reboarded the boat. They were heading north. One of the experts asked him what the goal of his trip was. Awad ignored him and closed his eyes, recalling Shindi's words: *My land, my land.* As they progressed north, the villages slipped farther away, disappearing, and he was disappearing, too, and vanishing from existence. He only regained a sense of himself as the stupendous edifice loomed: the dam. He felt a rush of anguish.

5

Awad arrived back in Aswan melancholy. He bought a bottle of arak and left the city quickly, by train, and drank and drank until nothing was left. He dropped off the train, reeling and singing *My land*. He found Shindi, who was also getting drunk alone under a slender palm tree; he would never stop singing until he died or went mad. They would never invite him to celebrations now that he had become a source of trouble. Awad passed him, and moved confusedly on. He found a wedding procession passing by, drums, trilling, and dancing. He stopped and watched angrily; the land was being drowned, and here they were merry. The procession passed before him with all its noise and dancing, and then, without knowing how, without realizing it, he was among them, clapping and singing madly, forgetting all his principles. The women were frightened and moved away from him, and the men pushed him away. He found himself outside the circle as the procession moved on. He sat down and wept from the pain of drunkenness and injustice.

6

The war had broken out at the wrong time, and he was a lone knight, without a shield to protect his chest, without even a specific objective. He slept a while with the Sleepers of the Cave and awoke too late. This was not the time to dig up history which required close study. They were not the ones who had destroyed the south and annihilated its knights. But he was filled with a rage that deprived him of any peace. This was a losing battle by any standard. He was facing a country bristling with arms, and the people of Nubia were so decent and forgetful that all they asked of the world was shelter and a good death. Even so, he roamed the villages and went into the schools, mosques, homes, and markets, meeting village headmen, sheikhs, teachers, and students, and getting them into discussions that always left him with a splitting headache. Not one of them knew any of their forgotten history or had any enthusiasm for it. Was he dreaming or was he crazy? The village mayor advised his mother, "The government is watching your son, Hushia. Try to make him see reason."

Hushia had had it with Awad. This was a strange boy, and nothing was stranger than his brain. She had made him amulets and buried them near where he slept and where he relieved himself. Jazuli offered Awad all his savings to open a business or get married. Abbas Tawfiq cautioned her, "Hushia, this is serious now. The town is full of disguised strangers, and they're all spies who go around asking for news of your son." He pointed out to her a seller of skins and pelts, a clover peddler, and a cobbler, and swore to her by the Prophet's own faith that he knew one of them, who had winked at him and motioned him not to say anything; he had seen him once with the officer from the police station. Hushia was surprised by the idea of all these men following her son. What had he done? He was not a killer or a thief; he had not done anyone out of their money or fled from military service or taken over government land. She did not believe what Abbas Tawfiq was saying, and went straight to the clover peddler and, in her naiveté and foolishness, asked if he really were a peddler, or a *misi kol*—an informer. A student passing by happened to hear her and drew her far away. He told her, "Auntie Hushia, informers don't announce themselves." But her question made the rounds as a joke and made everyone laugh at a time when people treasured laughter. "Did you hear what Hushia al-Nur told the peddler? She swore she wouldn't buy from him until he told the truth—was he a clover peddler or a *misi kol*?" The people in Qirshah and the neighboring villages stopped their chatter. When they did talk, they resorted to their puzzling Nubian tongue. They stopped gathering in public and visiting the market or the station unless absolutely necessary. All the *misi kol* strangers were white. The principal of the school, Ibrahim Idun, said that the government had sent him one teacher more than he needed, and when he went to the regional office to clear it up, they told him those were the orders from above. Abdu Shindi was the only one who picked a fight with the suspects. Whenever he saw any one of them he told him loudly, to make people laugh, "How are you, *hanwa dol*?" But even he ceased his serious joking after one of the strangers attacked him and beat him nearly to death. He made it clear to him that he was not a northerner, in spite of his light complexion—he was a southerner born of a Cairene mother and understood Nubian perfectly. But the words *hanwa dol* (big jackass) stuck to the spies even more than *misi kol* had. After Friday prayers, the people talked of nothing but the calamity they had been enduring since the arrival of Hushia's son. They agreed to meet in the mayor's house after evening prayers, as was their custom whenever there was someone they needed to talk and seek advice about. They drank tea and passed around cigarettes and discussed several topics before getting around to the topic of the day, the story of Awad Shalali, who would bring sixty more calamities upon the people. The atmosphere of the meeting darkened with the appearance of Demerdash—who had not been invited—because he was a drunkard and extremist, and had nothing to contribute to any serious meeting. He made his living smuggling and from the pockets of the returning expatriates, and had a sharp tongue. They returned his greeting coolly and resumed their debate.

"This Awad Shalali, men—he's misguided, and he misleads others."

"He's poisoning the children's minds."

"Are we what he calls us?"

"He wants us to fight the government."

"We have to do something—tonight."

"Imagine—my worthless son says we're to blame for all the trouble!"

"What trouble?"

"Agreeing to be resettled."

"That's what Hushia's son says."

"So what do we do, people?"

"Let the mayor deal with him."

Demerdash spoke after a long silence, jarring them.

"Listen to you! Hushia's son is an educated man, and he wants what's best for you."

"What's best for whom?" snapped Haj Ahmad Abbas. "He doesn't pray, and he has not fulfilled half of his faith, as you've done—he hasn't married."

"What does praying or marriage have to do with this?" exclaimed Demerdash angrily. "We have people here who've made the pilgrimage to Mecca, and they'd still steal the Prophet's own money—they'd steal the Prophet himself if he weren't nailed down."

"Stop it! Shame on you, Demerdash!" several voices interrupted.

"Don't offend your own uncles and relatives who are here."

"We are your elders."

"And your betters!"

"You little shit!"

Demerdash endured the stream of insults and replied, calmly and sadly:

"Listen, the man is only asking that we get some good agricultural land and reasonable compensation."

"That's the responsibility of our officials and the parliament and the Nubian organizations in Cairo."

Demerdash's voice rose to a scream in interruption:

"Officials and the government! What good do they do us? Nubian organizations! They can go to hell! What's their job but to build tombs and bury the dead? What do they give us, a few cents? Has your cowardice reached the point where you'd plot against one of our own people? I despise you!"

The mayor rushed at Demerdash with his cane, but was held back. They cursed and taunted one another, they scolded one another, then read the *Fatiha* together to make up, and then recited the formulas "There is no power or strength save in God," "In the name of God, the compassionate, the merciful," and "I seek refuge in God from accursed Satan," and then the discussion resumed.

"Listen, Demerdash," said Haj Ahmad Abbas. "This boy is really crazy. Yesterday he came to me and told me, 'Haj, you are an enlightened man, and you have opinions, and people trust you. You have to help enlighten the people, and then you talk to me in puzzles and riddles,' and I came away from all that with the feeling that I was in the presence of a lunatic."

"What did he say to you, Haj?"

"All nonsense, like the state of Nubia and the 'bowmen of the glance' and Kashta and Taharka and Dongola, and names and subjects that would make your head spin."

"What do we have to do with this Dongola?"

"He says it was the capital of the Christian state of Nubia."

"Oh, no! Were we Christians, too?"

"That's what he says."

"God help us."

"We have always been Muslims and believed in only one God."

"That infidel!"

"The whole family is crazy."

"Listen, everyone, the best solution is to banish him."

"Expel him? From his own country?" gasped Demerdash. "God damn you all."

"You are the damned one, you lazy fool."

"Watch it, Demerdash."

Demerdash rebuked them:

"Understand me, people, we have to stand by Awad Shalali, and support him."

"In what?"

"Our rights, people."

"So we should fight the government, Demerdash? You have

no one, Demerdash. You have no wife, no child, no job—this is the first time we've seen you worked up about anything. But about something bad!"

"I swear to God," Demerdash mocked him, "you people are the biggest cowards on earth."

"What about you?"

"Give me a gun and I'll show you."

"You're a talker, that's all," sneered the mayor, and then alluded to an old incident. "You see a camel whip and take to your heels. And if you aren't ashamed, say what you want. Where do you think you are, Nakhlat Ali Shami?"

Haj Ahmad Abbas left his stern dignity behind and coughed long and hard, and there was an explosion of laughter behind him, as the men on the banks of the Nile always did at the mention of Nakhlat Ali Shami, which brought them back to their former brooks, palms, the small hamlets, graveyards, and old tales. Back then, Demerdash had been a bold and insolent young man plying his boat to move smuggled goods between the cataracts and Halfa, running around both countries' customs authorities. His daring was a matter of record: he skirmished with crocodiles, swam in the river challenging its whirlpools, hunted snakes or scorpions; he traveled through the villages by night, alone, wrestling the local youth and always winning. It was said that he could even intimidate the djinn that dwelt in the ruins and temples. One night when they were at a wedding in the village of Maria, he made a bet with the other men of his age that he could go the distance between the two villages, at night, alone with his mule and his staff to frighten away wolves. The men heard of the bet and intervened, scolding him, giving advice, and trying to restrain him. But he had his way. As soon as he left the shelter of the barking dogs, he was attacked by an army of hungry wolves until all the wolves of the south had gathered in a pack behind him. He recalled that they were afraid of fire, so he set his turban on fire, and then his robe, and then his underpants. He was barely able to reach Nakhlat Ali Shami, leaving his mule to the savage beasts. The men who raced to save him found him up a palm tree, naked, and he had shit on himself. From that day on they called him al-Zurat, which meant the boaster and the shitter, which made him quiet down and stop engaging in lunatic behavior. As to the camel whip, there was no one in the land of Nubia who did not fear him after they had been tamed by dozens of raids; now the son of a terrified generation saluted to the military officers even before the soldiers did. The old people told stories they had heard from their grandparents, and from their ancestors, horrible stories of long lines of soldiers marching south, destroying everything in their path, and anyone who fell into their hands was taken captive and sold into slavery. The people fled to the mountains with their children and their livestock until the danger was past. Those hard days had taught them obedience to the government, whether it was tyrannical or just. After silencing Demerdash, the mayor raised his voice, and there was no opposition: "Listen. God's people! This boy, Hushia's son, is mad—totally mad. How can he incite us against a government that moved us from the mountains and saved us from starvation, which gave us ready-made houses and compensation? They celebrated our coming and built us schools and hospitals. We are not ungrateful people. Have you forgotten what the kings, sultans, and the English did after the Aswan reservoir was built? Why does he want us to fight the very people who stood by us? Why is that necessary? The people of Egypt are our people. They share our faith, and they feed us, and the Prophet's own family members are buried there. This Dongola he preaches about—all its men are the doormen of Cairo! They're hungrier than we are! The present ruler of Egypt is an Upper Egyptian, and a brave man, and we Kanzis are the close relatives of the Upper Egyptians. Look what this man has given us: clean water, electricity, and security. We should all thank God!"

"Well said, sir."

"That is the truth."

"Wise words for whomever will listen."

"I feel like we're listening to the radio—to 'Voice of the Arabs from Cairo,'" laughed Demerdash mockingly.

"Brother, leave us alone," said the mayor testily. "You can listen to the BBC if you prefer."

Haj Ahmad Abbas spoke up to end this overlong discussion.

"We all should thank God. Let anyone listen to what he likes. Let us have some tea. Let us recite the *Fatiha,* Muslims."

While they were arguing and reciting the *Fatiha,* police cars had encircled Hushia al-Nur's house and the roads leading into the village. Soldiers deployed inside the house, searching for Awad Shalali and for nonexistent leaflets and weapons. They heard Hushia scream, and before anyone could be sent to get news, Abbas Tawfiq appeared, shaking and upset, to inform the village mayor what had happened. The men slipped back, hidden by the darkness. Because of his job, the mayor went to see the visitors, and the chief of the force told him threateningly:

"You are the village mayor, and you have to bring us Awad Shalali immediately, no matter where he is." Demerdash was the only one among the terrified citizenry of the village who had courage before the visitors; he stood unintimidated, wanting to do something, though he could not, because the force was numerous, and their weapons were drawn. The mayor stood trembling, almost pissing with fear. He begged Hushia to tell them where her son was, and she swore to him that Awad had gone to Aswan. Demerdash burned with shame as he watched the soldiers insulting Hushia and her brother, throwing them into the police wagon like sacks of meal. He inwardly cursed the government and the people of the village. When the top-ranking officer saw him, he ordered him away contemptuously: "Get out of here! Go play somewhere else, boy." Demerdash took a step toward him and answered boldly: "I am a man, not a boy."

"Take him! Take this son of a bitch!" shouted the officer angrily.

When a soldier approached him to put him in the police wagon, he retreated, cursing in Nubian, curses so obscene that had the officer understood, he would have ordered him shot on the spot. The mayor was surprised by the strength of Demerdash's steadfastness and by his reply to the senior officer. After all, when this officer barked an order in Aswan, his subordinates trembled as far away as Kom Ombo. But what Demerdash did next became a story recounted with amazement and respect.

7

Demerdash, who had been described as a coward, withdrew to his house and slept peacefully after cursing the visitors in a language they did not know. The story needed not the slightest commentary, because insulting an outsider in Nubian was scarcely a heroic act; the women did it all the time to outsiders and peddlers when they were harassed or cheated. But he was in an intense rage when the officer cursed him and addressed him as "boy," though he was a grown man. Even worse was the insult to Hushia al-Nur, right in front of the mayor's eyes. If they had done that with an Upper Egyptian woman, the whole contingent of police would have been annihilated. He wished he'd had a gun with him that night. He thought the best way of getting back at those arrogant men was to make sure their mission was a failure. So he decided to save the courageous boy Awad Shalali and keep him out of their hands. But how, when he did not know where he was? He thought, if he is in Aswan, and coming back tonight, he will have to come in a shared taxi, because the last train had headed north two hours ago. Despite the troops deployed and the *misi kol*, he slipped out and went out to hide beside the road, in the place where the taxis stopped to let out the passengers for this village. Only chance, and the government's bad luck, made Awad Shalali's taxi stop a few yards away from him. He ran to him and embraced him, pulled him behind an abandoned building, and convinced him not to turn himself in to those dogs. They ran through the side streets and discussed it. They thought it over. They debated. He learned why the government was so upset: he had called for a youth meeting that was to have been held the next day in the village of Kalabshah. Demerdash thought about how to protect this boy and found a solution. He headed for the village of Salwa and knocked at the door of his fellow vagrant and drinking partner, Rabi al-Salwawi. After greeting him, he said, "Listen, Rabi—Salwawi, we've come to find safety with you. We've run, because I don't know a better man than you. You are sensible and lucky, and the best man around, because you're Jaafari and Ansari, and this guy is a great guy, like you. Can you hide him and protect him? What do you say?"

Rabi al-Salwawi saluted by placing his fist beside his neck, and said, "Whatever you say. You and your guest are welcome here before I know who your guest is and what he's done. You have my word." He called his sleeping wife and ordered her to prepare the finest food they had to offer their guests. He found a lamb and slaughtered it. "Welcome, welcome, Kanzis!" he said happily. "My family and I are all at your command. My grandfather, God rest his soul, wanted me to look after you. He said that one time he killed a Turkish tax collector and fled to Nubia. He stayed there and was treated well, and now I can repay the favor with you." He took his rifle from its hiding place, loaded it, and said, "Demerdash, from now on no one is going to harm your guest except over my dead body." For several days Demerdash moved between the village of Salwa in Kom Ombo, and Qirshah and Daraw. He talked to Basharis and caravans and his informants, and with great effort was finally able to make a deal to leave. Their story was still a secret, until one of four, Hushia al-Nur, her brother Jazuli, or perhaps Rabi al-Salwawi, revealed the details. It may have been Demerdash himself who got drunk and let the secret slip while boasting.

8

It was night when they left. They branched off east of the Aswan reservoir, and followed unpaved roads far from the Nile. They went deep into the mountains, climbed boulders, and crossed valleys. Their objective was Wadi Dahmit; there they would rest and take on another guide who would take them on an escape route to Abu Hamad; they would split up once inside Sudan. Awad Shalali, the escapee, the fugitive, had made a break from his whole past, both sweet and bitter, both south and north. He was heading into the heartland of "the bowmen of the glance," the extreme south. He knew nothing of the day to come; his chief concern was to flee from the ogre of arrest, which had pursued him for ten years. He wore Bashari clothes as a laughable form of camouflage: leather sandals, a white robe with rear pockets, a high turban, and a whip. He had a few words of Sudanese he had learned quickly, to give quick answers. His traveling companions were Nubian youths, mostly high school graduates who had ended their studies; instead of enlisting in the army, they chose to flee, preferring that to the army recruitment camp at Munqabad. They did not have an antigovernment position, wanting only jobs and money in the oil states, which they entered with Sudanese passports that helped them to move smoothly between the kingdoms and sheikhdoms.

Shortly before dawn, the expert Bashari guide called out and squinted warningly: "Let me check this out, man," he said. They stopped and then sat down and listened anxiously, prepared to fight or run. The guide ran ahead on his own, scanning the ground, and looking into Wadi Dahmit from above. He returned at sunup, scowling. "There's no talk, no noise—they're all sleeping." They learned from him that the camel-borne soldiers were in an ambush at the well and would not trouble them until they set out to hunt the fugitives. The agreement between the two guides at the well and the tour around the Wadi took time and effort. They slept. They worried. They got up, ate, and thought things over. They got bored. Then, out of patience, they decided to cross the Wadi by night. The experienced guide did not agree, because the camels would leave tracks with the dawn, and they could be followed by the fast government camels. They were his own responsibility, because the sons of his friends and Demerdash's friends were among the fugitives. On the morning of the next day, when the guides were to meet, nothing had changed. They thought through every possibility except turning back. They briefly considered retreating and voluntarily turning themselves in at Munqabad as being preferable to returning under escort. The guide joined in, saying, "If you have extra cash, I'll go give them a bribe." But how much of a bribe, Bashari? They talked it over and pooled their extra money. "It's not enough. More." Awad Shalali handed over more. The guide sped down the Wadi, lightly and briskly, carefully and apprehensively observed; they watched him sit with the soldiers. He talked with them and drank tea. The Bashari came back after the success of his bribing mission. How much had he paid them? Had he split the money with them? Had he deceived both sides? But Awad Shalali trusted him; these were the sort of men who did not bargain or lie. The desert and the truth. If he had said no . . . he could not be forced to give in. If he grew angry, he would draw his sword and cut someone's head off. Rabi al-Salwawi had been formed by his surroundings, his nights, his ready sword. Such men were rare. They were like boulders; they stood by their word. To what vile race did that informer belong? It was a bewildering question, for he had never been able to understand the mentality of the northerners; some of them were so brilliant as to be virtual prophets, while others were the lowest of the low. What kind of people were they? They watched the soldiers crowded brazenly around the well and the whole Wadi. The two guides met, embraced, and spoke in Nubian, and the exchange was made. They were now the responsibility of the new guide, Jah al-Rasul al-Jinn—"messenger of the demons"— as he called himself, a desert devil whose heart was of granite. He was expert on the south and an expert tracker. He devised new paths through the towering heights and steep valleys. He climbed mountains and flew over easy ground, singing songs they did not understand. This hero was a descendant of the Bajaou who had scouted this region long ago, who had spread into Nubia, Aswan, and Upper Egypt, fighting bloody battles with the Arabs. They conquered, accepted Islam, and divided into the Ababidah and the Basharis. The Basharis had retained their horsemanship, swords, and strength, while the Ababidah and the people of Nubia had surrendered and changed. They reached the well called Umm Ashara and sat there to rest. "Demerdash is one of a kind," thought Awad Shalali. "He risked his life and his brother's." He had hidden him and managed his escape, though he belonged to the rival tribe of Miknab, and they had no special link. They had not played together as boys or been schoolmates. Awad was a Kanzi, a Nubian, a Qirshawi. Where was Demerdash? And yet in adversity he showed his mettle. There must be others like him, and he had to search them out. Accursed fear kept them in the dark, a terrible inherited chronic fear. Perhaps the most daring thing Demerdash did was the meeting he arranged for Awad with his mother and uncle the night of his escape. His mother was a broken woman and spoke falteringly.

"Shame on you, Nephew," his uncle scolded him. "Your mother cannot sleep."

"This is my fate."

"We gave you advice."

"What did they do to you?"

"You know how they are."

"What did they do?"

"They held me for two days and beat me, and they insulted your mother."

"The dogs!"

"They still patrol the village."

"I left it to them."

"They might remove the mayor."

"What difference would that make?"

"We want to make sure you're all right."

"Think of my mother."

"Don't worry about her. I have enough money to last us our whole lives. Look after yourself."

Hushia clung fast to him and refused to let go.

"We have no time, Hushia," said Demerdash. "Your son is a man—the best man of all."

"*Adila*," she said, meaning goodbye.

"Goodbye. Go to our people in Halfa and Dongola."

Where was Dongola? Where was Halfa? What city was populated? Was there any salvation from this rough, deadly path? The first to make his way through this wasteland must have been pursued by something even worse, death probably. "What drove you to such bitterness?" Yes, choice and misery. The bones of camels which perished of exhaustion or which had fallen from above. A scattered human skeleton, its fate written on its bones: wolves. Did Jah al-Rasul al-Jinn know his secret? Would he sell him to the camel riders? A Bashari would not betray him. If only he had an army of them! They understood chivalry and loyalty. They approached the well of Muraqah and met with an Ababidah caravan accompanied by a woman who had been bitten by a viper. They had been unable to treat her with herbs, bloodletting, or supplications to Sheikh Shazli, and they were now on their way to the countryside, to Daraw or Aswan. Where did these people live? What did they eat and drink? What deadly isolation had they chosen for themselves? Was it the asceticism of prophets, or the hiding place of miscreants? Was it the fear of contamination from the plagues of the city, or the attachment to their environment and special identity? The Nubians, the Ababidah, the Basharis, the desert Arabs, the people of the Siwa Oasis, and the wandering gypsies—what if he sat among them and taught them, and civilized them? Would that not be a noble calling, assuming that nobility was his aim? But prophecy was a hard calling, and he had given ten years of his life to a cause he had seen as noble. To stay in this vast wasteland to be bitten by a viper lurking below a layer of sand, to eat food made from camel milk and seasonal pigeons, and to sacrifice all the achievements of civilization, would be too much even for a saint. If he were to get the courage to do it, the first thing he would have to do would be to gather the people together of the tribe and tell them frankly, "Brothers, I have come to tell you that Sheikh Shazli, whose shrine you spend long days making pilgrimage to, so that he may bless you, is just a fairy tale." Then what response could await him other than the sword? Shazli, Mursi, Abu al-Abbas, Sayyid al-Badawi, the lady, and the Lord. In every village and city was a huge lie called protection: they described Egypt as *al-Mahrusah,* "the protected," because its territory held the burial places of the Prophet's family members —and yet Egypt had always been invaded and defeated. The sheikhs, fairy tales, and worries of Awad Shalali. Now his friends were blessed with jobs in journalism, and those who had been with him in the Qurtah school were now principals in the schools of Nubia. He was an outcast, a fugitive. The day they made him a teacher in the Qirshah school, succeeding a northern teacher, the village was overjoyed. His mother gave a party, and they gave her the title Umm al-Ustaz, the teacher's mother. It gave her new importance and prestige. When they asked him to address the worshipers at the mosque on Friday, he horrified them by giving a sermon attacking their values and beliefs, and even the shrine of Sheikh Abd al-Rahim, which he described as a remnant of paganism. They were alarmed and avoided asking his views on religious values. His mother filled the house with incense and prayed, "O Sheikh Abd al-Rahim, forgive him for my sake," and she made an offering of a lamb for him. This deluded Bashari guide had lost his right mind and his instinctive caution and led them both into a lethal pothole, crossing into Wadi Alaqi in daylight. They were surrounded by a border patrol headed by a sharp old southern sergeant assisted by an even sharper Bashari guide. They were pursuing some smugglers, but the distance between them and their prey had widened, and they were afraid of the desert and running out of supplies. What would happen now? The guides embraced one another and spoke in Nubian, exchanging family news. Then they sat whispering while the soldiers made the camels kneel and spread out to gather fire-wood to make tea and *duka* bread, made on a tin sheet. Despite his humble rank, the sergeant now ruled this tiny corner of the world. He was not a peacock, like a northern officer, but simple and humble. He jokingly smacked them on the face or the back of the neck; it was not a hard slap or a tender pat. He gave advice and asked questions as a father would: "Why did you leave the country to go wandering, boys?" He looked over their identification cards and asked about their home towns and family origins. Terribly alarmed, Awad Shalali put all his energy into giving convincing answers, because he was the eldest of the fugitives, and his presence among the other young men looked odd. And in fact the sergeant selected him and took him aside, far from the others; he sat cross-legged and asked Awad to sit. He put a plug of chewing tobacco into his toothless mouth and stared straight at Awad, who was thinking that perhaps this man could act as an intermediary in the matter of the bribe. He prepared himself to maneuver and bargain. The sergeant chewed the tobacco and traced lines in the sand with his index finger:

"Where is my brother from?"

"Nubia."

The sergeant laughed and spat out some juice.

"Do you think I took you for English? I mean, what place are you from?"

"I am Kanzi."

"I know that, my boy. I'm asking about your village, not your background."

"Qirshah."

"Son of whom?"

"Do you know everyone in my village?"

"I come from the Arabs of your country. We lived in the last village in old Nubia, and now our houses are mingled with those of the resettlement."

"Welcome."

"We may turn out to be related."

"I'm the son of Shalali of Naj al-Alyab."

"You are the Awad who—" The sergeant wiped the traces of tobacco from his lips and added calmly, "We have a bulletin about you in the tribal area center."

Had they also alerted the airports, seaports, Interpol, and friendly governments? Did he know all this? Was it not enough for him that he had left the battlefield to them? There was no way this sergeant wished him well. He was from an isolated Arab hamlet, far from the villages of Qirshah, one of the descendants of the Rubi'a tribes which had invaded northern Nubia. When he was young he used to get into rock-throwing fights with their children and call them "dirty Arabs." It is true that they were usually good neighbors, but the old psychological barrier still remained. They had retained their Arab language, and kept their distance, and kept to themselves, and felt themselves to be the masters. This guide—was he a conspirator? He was still whispering with the government guide. If he ran for it, his back would be exposed to the bullets of the old Lee-Enfield rifles. Should he take a risk and offer a bribe before they requested it? Once Demerdash had saved him, and the good behavior of his previous guide. Who would save him the third time? Should he raise his hands to the heavens in supplication? Should he throw himself at the sergeant's feet and beg him not to do his duty, only because he had been truthful with him? Should he bribe him? God help him from the judges of the north, who would make him an example to all rebels and dissidents. His old comrades would not stand by him, and the Nubians would condemn his ideas. He had to flee or die here. The sergeant stood up, dusting off his uniform.

"Your grandfather was one of the sheikhs of Nubia. But you and your father—may God guide you, my boy. Tell the people of Alyab, 'I met Sirr al-Khatm in the desert.'"

Then he lightly mounted his kneeling camel and said mysteriously, "You'll be seeing someone else." Awad Shalali was stilled stunned; this man had decided not to do his duty and was giving up an easy promotion without asking anything in return. Awad could think of no explanation except that he was lucky, and it was he who was always looking for reasons.

The two caravans parted, and the guide began to sing, in Sudanese this time: "They lost it and knew it—you do not know your friend from your enemy. God will give you your rights and punish those who oppressed you." Oppression and loss, and nonexistent rights. Why had the sergeant left him alone? Had the guide bribed him? Or because they were on another mission? Awad Shalali approached the guide.

"Your friends?"

"The whole desert knows me, even the red devils."

"How did you get rid of them?"

"I am Jah al-Rasul and no one gets the better of me."

"Even patrols of government spies?"

"Even from the devil himself. I could get rid of him for

you." Then he brandished his sword and added, "I'm the prophet of the desert, and the Basharis' best man!"

The young men muttered a prayer of contrition for this blasphemy and said the prayer of the fearful. This rough, instinctive guide was neither a believer nor a pagan, nor was he vain. He was just expressing his confidence in himself and his way of doing his work.

But the young men with Awad were worried now, and one of them raised his hand and said pleadingly, "He is ignorant, Lord! Forgive him for our sake!"

"How did we end up with this madman?" another asked angrily.

If the Deity were to get angry with the guide, would the others accept his sin? If the guide were suddenly to die, would they die soon after in this wasteland? Didn't the guide, the captain, the navigator, and the commander need the logic of things as an alternative? Refuge from the sun was crevices or caves. The people who lived here or passed through would not take refuge in the fires of hell.

"Get up, Jah al-Rasul," said a youth who had just finished praying, and who was losing his mind. "Say a prayer and ask forgiveness."

He also said to Awad, who was thinking aloud, "And you, Awad Shalali, why don't you pray?"

If prayer were the refuge from the oppression of the world, he would have prayed, but the men who had maimed the people of Nubia and sold them as slaves also prayed. The murderers of the caliphs and princes had also prayed. The guide cared nothing for these fearful people or the burning sun, but kept watching the far horizon, trying to establish the distance that remained to Wadi Jarib and Bir Arifta—names and places that did not exist on maps. Sometimes he turned back to examine tracks closely, to see whether they had been left by camel riders or local people; the track told him everything. How many times had he crossed this hell, venturing out or coming home? Executioners, snake charmers, wild animal tamers, divers, pimps, and mercenary soldiers . . . was there no other way to earn a living? Awad Shalali's thoughts were still far away, analyzing the meaning behind the behavior of Sergeant Sirr al-Khatm, the descendant of the invading Rubi'a tribe. Was he like Demerdash, Rabi al-Salwawi, and Shindi, all of whom might have belonged to a secret group he did not know of, with the common goal of reviving chivalry and gallantry? Or else the guide had a special, obscure relationship with the border police. But it was the guide who had asked about the conversation between Awad and the sergeant. He was too preoccupied to answer. He repeated the question: "What's the story?"

"I have no idea."

"You know him?"

"No."

The guide was as bewildered as he was; he said, worriedly, "Who are you?" If Awad knew who he himself was, he would tell him. After breaking off from his past, would he be able to learn who he was? At Bir Arifta, they found a dead Nubian fugitive. They washed and buried him, and the guide said he had drunk after an intense thirst. They filled their water flasks and water bags with stinking water and moved on. They stopped when the guide espied thick dust on the horizon which he thought might be a border police vehicle, though it turned out to be blowing sand which then settled. Reassured that all was well, the guide resumed singing in the Bashari language, and the Nubians imitated him in their own language. What was the origin of these languages? Were they related to the language of ancient Egypt? The voice of a Nubian youth rose, chanting Abdu Shindi's latest lament:

> "Nubia, my homeland,
> Land of my fathers, my palm trees
> Secret of my sorrows! My land, farewell."

Yes—farewell to Nubia. Awad Shalali was leaving thirty-nine villages behind him. He was defeated. This was an exodus of the vanquished. He listened to the chanting, which had become a wail.

"My homeland . . ."

He wanted to sing, too. He opened his mouth: "My ho . . ." His voice broke, and he choked. He collapsed into a sitting position. He put his hand on his head, as mourning women did.

"What's wrong, man?" asked the guide, surprised.

"Toothache," he lied.

"Men don't cry!"

Yes. They did not cry. They were cast out, imprisoned, or banished. Then scoundrels and traitors were rewarded with jobs, glory, and peace of mind.

They moved on, grew weary, slept, and got up. The most purposeful and eager to arrive was Awad Shalali. After thirteen days of hardship, the guide announced happily, "Good news, men! We're here." They looked ahead expectantly but saw no dwellings or any sign of life. This was merely the imaginary borderline which he knew by landmarks. They still had a journey of a full day and night before reaching Abu Hamad.

PART TWO

The Trial of Awad Shalali

1

One hour before the arrival of the train from the north, the platform at Kalabshah Station was crowded with well-wishers, flatterers, and dreamers. The newcomer may have been an expatriate being received by the men and women of the entire village. Perhaps no one would come, with only rumors and dreams occupying the station platform with the movement of the train south. The life of these people, which consisted of perpetually waiting for absent people scattered all through the world seeking the livelihoods lacking here, had changed. They had been quickly dispersed and discarded at the base of Silsilah Mountain, middle-aged people and widows. They were granted small allowances, and the able-bodied were left idle and loitering, and so they left on an essential migration, leaving their mothers and wives behind to guard the stone houses in what was called their new homeland.

Hushia al-Nur could stand only with difficulty, leaning against the wall and her cane, straining to hear the footsteps of the people rushing to the station, asking the pedestrians her daily question: "Tell me, people! Who has come?"

"God knows."

"Is it Hasan Madani?"

"Maybe."

"Please tell me."

"Maybe it's your son, Hushia."

"Please, Lord."

Please, Lord, she sighed, *Please, Lord*. She lifted her palms to beseech the heavens. *Please, Lord, make me patient*. Her life was worry, hope, and dreams, and her patience surpassed that of any saint. For nine years she had dreamed of the impossible, of he who did not come, whose whereabouts she did not know. She searched for him in the eyes and the memories of the returnees. A fortuneteller had predicted good news, and she believed him. She heard the women trilling with joy and grew sad. She cried. She went to each new arrival, wherever he was—the villages were filthy and far away—and all the returned expatriates knew the story of her vanished son. They pitied her and listened guardedly to her questions, but they did not have the answer she wanted. She asked questions and they prevaricated.

"Did you look for my son, Hasan Madani?"

"Wherever I went, by God, Aunt."

"What is the news?"

He said nothing. She understood, grew sad, and cried. She went to another returnee before resting from the weariness of her journey.

"You, Sabir Abd al-Rahim, where were you?"

"Kuwait."

"Give me good news."

"May God bring him back safely."

"And you, Abd al-Ghafur?"

"I asked about him all over the Hejaz, I swear, Aunt."

"What did they say?"

"I wish I had heard some good news."

The last place she journeyed to was the village of Tushki.

"You spent a long time abroad, dear boy."

"I visited everywhere."

"Did you hear of Awad Shalali?"

"The fact is, I don't think your son is in the Arab countries."

"Where could he be?"

"What I heard from people—"

"May it be good news you heard, God willing!"

"That he—"

"Yes?"

"Was in a foreign country."

In what foreign country? she wondered. Was he not in some Muslim land? Was he in the land of Gog and Magog? She began to ask questions and investigate, closely following the news of returnees until one day she heard of someone who had been in a foreign country. It was her last hope. She sought him out impatiently but was patient for years, and she grieved at the puzzling report the man gave her: "The foreign countries, Lady Hushia, are not like our old lands, where everyone is related by family and language and religion, like a sailing ship where you stroll the deck for a few days, and the people in it know one another and visit one another. It is a vast land, Lady Hushia, very large, and occupies the three continents. They travel there in huge ships, planes, and trains. The oceans separate them, and they speak several languages. The people living in one street, even in the same building, don't know one another, and they hardly greet one another. In which country does your son live?"

"My boy, I swear by God I didn't understand one word you said."

THE TRIAL OF AWAD SHALALI 63

"Lady Hushia—"

"Tell me the truth, my boy. You were there?"

"Yes, in Rome."

"And that place, isn't that in that terrible country?"

"A country of a thousand—"

"In that horrible land?"

"Yes, but—"

"My son is dead. Dead, people! Dead!" She began to sob.

"Don't worry."

She threw dirt on her head and wailed and cursed the government and the world. They led her back to her house exhausted and lamenting. The women stood at their doors, curious and prepared to help, clutching their black wraps, trying to establish the facts before starting their procession to the house of the bereaved for mass mourning.

"God help us! Who is it?"

"Hushia al-Nur."

"Is she dead?"

"If only she were! We'd be rid of her and her bad luck!"

The joys and sorrows of the land of Nubia sparked off shouts or trills of happiness. There were forty days for receiving condolences and wearing black, and unending celebration before anyone's wedding night. There were special rituals for every occasion: for circumcision, childbirth, and illness. The women in the Kanz villages left the prisons of their houses only to offer condolences or congratulations. They could turn a scorpion sting into a funeral or the return of a migrant into a lavish celebration. Hushia al-Nur's shriek gathered them for condolences, and they sat around her united and vocal. They came with pitchers of tea and sat down to cry and chat. Each of them had some experience with treacherous fate, the unruliness of children, the emigration of husbands, a scarcity of food, the meager allowance they were paid, which scarcely could have fed an infant, publicly taking from the shop of Haj Ahmad Abbas and his ledger filled with the names of those who could not pay, and like them, Hushia al-Nur had long experience with fate.

2

Unknown to her, it was the day the northerners built their first reservoir at their southernmost city, rather than before it. She was a girl at the time of the second elevation of the reservoir, but she experienced every detail of the catastrophe: the river that rose up, swallowing the houses and the small strip of land that had survived the first elevation, and flooding the greater part of their agricultural land. This time it encompassed the mountain and poured like a nightmare over the heart of the south, bringing its punishment upon them—they who had loved it, sung to it, and even deified it long ago. It did not aim its blow at the northerners who had prevented its spread and mocked it in their "bride of the Nile" rites. The people of Nubia opened their eyes one day and the river was before them, their villages in its belly, and the mountain behind them. They sat and counted the compensation money and sighed. Those who despaired emigrated north. The strong and the steadfast were determined to stay. "We will never leave our land," they said. "We will build our new houses on the mountain and wait." Those who stayed endured a long winter, until the northerners opened the streams of the Aswan reservoir to release the stored water, for the water to burst in exhilaration into its historic course. The land was submerged, and joy filled the country. Sacrificial animals were slaughtered, and the mosques were brilliantly illuminated. Pious people visited shrines to give thanks, and everyone prayed. They praised the lord of the river. Long-delayed celebrations now took place. They planted, and the sorghum stalks rose up, amid the spreading fragrance of honeydew melons and watermelons. The days passed and harvest approached; they woke up and found the river rumbling and heading for the mountain. They raised their voices to God to deliver them, and they sought shelter in the mosques. They invoked ruin on the reservoir and the people of the north. A delegation of Arabic speakers went to Aswan to find out what the story was with the reservoir outlets which opened and closed with no warning, but they came home frustrated and defeated. When they took the compensation money, the land became state property, and by sowing in the summer they had committed an infraction. They had no right to do that. Most of the men left, looking for work. They sent money orders and packages home to their families. The homeland zealots, proud of their roots, remained in their obstinacy and resisted the sterility, the game of the inundation, and the mysterious operation of the reservoir. Hushia's father was one of the most steadfast; he fished the river in winter and was the first to go out to the land as soon as the water receded. He waded into the mud and slime, devising ways to be the first to farm. It was an effort steeped in danger, because the ground was soft and unstable: an open graveyard. But the harvest was a rich one, whether they closed the reservoir openings at the set time or did it early to trap the flood water. Wiser heads advised him to think it over, because it was always safest to proceed slowly. But he laughed at them and kept planting, reaping, and selling, and he was able to live respectably. That is, until the day came which Hushia would never forget. It was after the dawn prayers when he went down to some land that had just begun to sprout, in the bottom-lands by the river. The second day he saw the sun. The land was firm in a few areas, and soft throughout most of it, but expanses of water had made them into islands separated from the shore by a muddy canal. He knew the land he owned down to the last inch: there was a small hill, here was an old irrigation ditch. His habit was to walk slowly, feeling the ground with his long staff, poking it into the surface to test its firmness. He had done this for years, tossing seeds from a distance into areas whose surface firmness he did not trust. He never failed or sank in until he got too used to his ways, grew careless, and forgot both his caution and his staff. His left foot sank into a hole and he fell, but when he tried to extricate himself, his right foot sank in as well. He fell in as though some demonic power wanted to draw him into perdition, and in moments he was trapped up to his waist, then up to his chest. He shouted for help: "Help, O God! Help, good people! O God!" But the demon of the river pulled him under and he sank further, past his shoulders. He raised his arms. Hushia was the first to hear him; she, her mother, and her brother ran to him. The whole town emptied and stood on the shore and saw his two spread hands, and then nothing. Hushia wept, hating the reservoir and the people of the north. When she grew a little older, they married her to a southerner who had come down from the north and returned there two months after their marriage, which resulted in one child. All the men came back to Nubia except for her husband; he had been possessed by a northern temptress with long eyelashes, who had had her long braids down to him, and the day she learned, she received the condolences to be the first to hold a funeral ceremony of the living and she added the women of the north to the list of people she hated. Years passed in which she suffered to educate her son so he became a teacher. How much she suffered on account of this absent but beloved son, from his childhood until he was lost in his love for the north. Every summer he rushed there, paying her no mind. When he came back, he talked about things she did not understand and books whose contents she could not imagine. Haj Ahmad Abbas told her that her son's brain had been corrupted by his visits to the north. He had stopped praying. She had to marry him off as soon as possible, before it was too late. She advised him of this, and he consented and chose a bride. Then he went on a trip to buy her some gifts, but did not return. Hushia sent a cable to her brother and her husband, and all her relatives, but to no avail. She wrote protests and petitions and went to the governor of Aswan, and she visited the sheikhs and prayed. They told her, "Your son has chosen to follow a dangerous road—he's mixed up in politics." She did not understand. The years passed her by, and she spent most of them in tears.

The northerners' need for water increased, and they built a huge dam to the south of the first reservoir, a stupendous mountain that would block up all the water, except for a measured amount, which would inundate all of Nubia, with its temples, mountains, and villages. The country's most massive evacuation began. Hushia al-Nur refused to leave: "You can beat me and drag me away, but I won't leave."

"Everyone is leaving, Hushia."

"I want to die in my own land."

"Hushia, please!"

"I will never go to the land of that snake!"

She was the last to leave. They carried her out by force and put her among women who held onto her and tried to calm her down. She would not submit until they persuaded her that the land they were being evacuated to was far from the land of the woman who had stolen her husband. She gave in, took a house, and the world smiled upon her when the government released her son after ten years. She saw this as a good omen in the land of her exile, but her crazy boy was not like the obedient sons who pleased their mothers. She had no idea what had afflicted his mind. He still spoke of the same bewildering matters, and the government was still after him. She was absolutely certain that Ruhia, the sterile woman her husband had married, had cast some demonic spell to affect his innermost mind. The mayor, who was a member of her tribe, told her sympathetically, "Hushia, your son's brain is still not right. He is a heretic." She was afraid that what had happened to Bahr Jazuli would happen to Awad, because the government had no mercy. One month, thirty days she counted one by one, from the day of his release, the whole government came seeking him. It was a black night she would never forget. The light-skinned young officer had pushed her and insulted her, and they took her to the police station. It was the first time in her life she actually experienced the crudeness of such filthy soldiers. The young soldier, that son of a laundress, grabbed his club and asked her, "Are you going to tell us where he is, or am I going to have to shove this in your . . . ?" What times were these? Was this the way a Muslim man addressed a Muslim woman? She spat on him and cursed him. She was secretly pleased that her son was giving all these people such a hard time. Were these not the same people as Ruhia? This was real gloom. They were making her suffer terribly, but she would leave them to the judgment of He who never slept or slumbered. Despite all the pressure, she endured until her son was released safely and he left for Sudan. That was nine years ago. Those who had traveled with him told her that he had arrived safely. Where had he gone? Had they lied to her? They were certainly hiding something. Perhaps the Basharis had cut his head off. Perhaps they had seized him and dragged him back to prison, or perhaps he had died of exhaustion and been eaten by dogs. "My son is dead, people! Dead! *Ya badilli!*" This meant, what a loss! "My dear Awad!"

"Hushia, be comforted!"

"Be patient, Hushia!"

The years passed and she made them all weep. She lost her father, her son, and her brother, and then she lost the blessing of eyesight. Her brother had been ill for three years with an incurable disease that cost him all his money and left her with no supporter or companion. She had known happiness and pleasure only once, in the old country, the day she received the news of her husband's death. She trilled with joy and danced, and spread the rumor that the northern woman had poisoned him, the bastard, after she fell for another man. He had not divorced her, nor had he ever sent her money or visited her. The years wore on but she never gave up hope. She was as patient as a camel and as steadfast as a mountain. She waited for nineteen years. She was always chasing the mailman and the telegraph office employee.

"Do I have a telegram, effendi?"

"Soon, God willing."

"Do I have a letter, dear?"

"A letter?" The mailman laughed and said to himself, "Who is going to send that old thing a letter?" But after nineteen years and one month, the miracle occurred: the earth opened and the fugitive appeared.

3

It was night when he returned after a miserable day filled with trains that clattered onward, unwilling to reward the waiting villages with a lone expatriate in the season so crowded with returnees. The pessimists justified this by saying that Hushia's misfortune had hurt them, too—she had an evil eye, they said, that could break rocks; with her bad luck and woe, she had eliminated her son and everyone else's sons. People withdrew early inside their houses when they sought excuses to stay up, song or lamentation. How had he come? They wondered. Rumors said he had come home by the western desert road from Sudan, the same he had used to flee. They said that the same river demon which had snatched his grandfather had also snatched him, but then released him out of pity for his poor mother. Sheikha Mabrouka claimed that the angels had mercy on good-hearted Hushia and sent her a likeness of her absent son. The truth is that he had not come by train as he always had; he had landed at Aswan Airport and taken a taxi that dropped him off at the village late at night. Hearing the loud horn of the taxi, Abbas Tawfiq quickly slipped out of his hiding place, adjusting his clothes, thinking this was the police or some other official.

"Is that Abbas Tawfiq, the government representative?" Awad called.

"Awad—the devil!"

They hugged one another tightly; the government and the leader of the renegades met again after long absence. The taxi driver honked again loudly and did not stop, and Abbas returned the salute by firing his American rifle. The desolate and melancholy night of Qirshah turned into a celebration whose likeness would never be seen again, a celebration like the ones held in old Nubia when the land appeared as the water receded after a long winter. Was this night and this man returning from the invisible world like the land, a mirage, a trick of the light? Hushia al-Nur was confused and really did think she was dreaming. She had heard the cries and the drums, and her son's name, and was sure that demons were toying with her as usual. She sat on her palm-frond bed, called an *anjareeb* in Nubia, rubbed her eyes, and said a brief prayer, and believed nothing she heard. When she shuffled to the door, he was on the other side, and pushed it open with his whole body, and then everyone was inside, all around her, congratulating her and enjoying the good news. But she refused to believe them until her arms were around Awad, and she felt him and spoke to him. She trilled with joy until she was hoarse. Qirshah forgot sleep, and the young men around Awad Shalali besieged him so they could hear his story, and all about the money he had made, and the reason for his long absence. They asked him questions and listened carefully, and he told them lies and jokes.

"What work do you do, Awad Shalali?"

"I work at sea."

"In boats?"

"You think I've been catching fish?"

"Or crocodiles!"

In the south, boats were the principal way of traveling between the opposing banks of the Nile in sunken Nubia. The sails spread in the face of the wind. The oars. He had, in fact, worked on a boat that was as long as the distance between Qirshah and Alaqi. It was a floating city with all the pleasures of life. His life on it was like a dream: he ate the most delicious foods and drank the finest liquor, was on easy terms with the most elegant women, and visited the most beautiful ports and islands. He dazzled his listeners just as he had been dazzled. But he was clever enough to keep silent about the miserable part of his journey: his visit to the Dongola of his dreams, and his failed effort to establish a unified Nubian front. He was nearly thrown into prison because the people of Dongola and Halfa knew nothing of their ancient history, just like the people of Egyptian Nubia, and they thought he might be an agent of northern intelligence who had come to subvert the unity of Sudan. His said nothing about reunion with his Sudanese comrades and his disagreement with them because they asked him to go back north and to struggle there; they did not understand the harshness of the ten years he had spent in detention and prison. He cursed the north, the south, Nubia, Dongola, and his comrades, and departed, fleeing the fire of the sun and the whole dark continent. He crossed the sea to get away from the ignorant talkers, swords, executioners, and the stifling of thought, seeking a foothold anywhere. For four years he was driven from eastern to western Europe and back again. He first went to some comradely countries, to Hungary and Poland, and found them to be like Cairo: overshadowed by the military and full of people speaking in fearful whispers. In the west, he was lost for months, sleeping in parks in London and in the Metro tunnels of Paris. He sold newspapers and picked grapes. He worked in bars. Then Berlin and Stockholm. He dodged the Rome police until they'd had enough and accompanied him to the airport and deported him. They were dark years, but he managed to save money, and he wanted to use it to obtain legal residence, to pay an English prostitute to join him in a sham marriage. But she fooled him instead and disappeared with the money in front of the church, or the marriage office—he did not even know which it was. It was a devastating moment. He had no money and no place to live, and he could not return penniless to his native land, that prison. But despite his homelessness and loss, he enjoyed the freedom; people in Europe were really living. It was a wonderful world which did not know the cruelty of traditions, the rule of the military, or vague, unstable laws. Everyone believed in what he wanted: communists, existentialists, atheists, Christians, and Jews—even homosexuals and prostitutes had a voice. Why should he go back to a land of terror? If you had a policeman for a friend, you feared no one. He continued to wander among the capitals, going eventually to Greece where good fortune led him to a rich Greek who was part owner of a beautiful ship. This man had first made money in Alexandria where he had owned a hotel and a brewery. A virtual army of southerners worked for him; they had been loyal, and he loved them and had fine memories of them.

"You're from Aswan?"

"Yes."

"Nubian, of course."

"People in Cairo sometimes mistake me for a Sudanese."

"Matoki or Fadja?"

Awad Shalali laughed in surprise at this precise knowledge of Nubian tribal areas; this Greek knew the Nubian homeland, and knew some of the Nubian language, and he pronounced it perfectly. He asked him about many people: a waiter, a doorman, a cook, and a driver. They had been close to him, and he was generous with them, even educating their children in Egyptian schools and then in universities abroad. The food and beverage director on the boat was one of these. The Greek asked about one of the Nubians he remembered, from whom he had not heard for twenty years.

"Do you know Othman Bashir?"

"Yes, God rest his soul," said Awad, though he had no idea
which Othman he was talking about. One quarter of all the men
of Nubia were named Othman. The two men chatted and laughed
and reached an understanding. He agreed to work on the boat,
and was given the freedom to choose whatever work he liked,
since he spoke three languages besides Arabic. The food and
beverage director sent him to the dining room and trained him
quickly. Awad was delighted and soon worked his way up to
captain.

The boys clustered around Awad wanted to know more
about his work. He told them proudly, but without going into
detail, "I'm a captain." They repeated after him, full of surprise
and envy, "A captain?"

They thought he had reached the military rank of captain,
commanding the crew of a warship, not imagining he worked in
a dining room—even though that rank was not easy to achieve,
and was well paid. He, in turn, asked them about the dear friends
he had once known: Abdu Shindi, for one. They replied that
alcohol had destroyed his brain; he now lived under the care of
a religious hospice.

"And Demerdash?"

"Listen, brother, stop asking us about all this misery and
tell us about white meat!"

From the very beginning they had been trying to turn the
conversation toward their main interest: women. Awad Shalali
moaned softly and fell silent because he was still in the midst of
the only love story of his desolate life. Simone was a beautiful
woman who had changed him and made him see the world
impartially; she was French, a professor of oriental history, of
average beauty, intellectually refined, a tolerant woman, an
opponent of fanaticism. She loved the whole world and detested
the idea of Western superiority. He met her on one of the inso-
lently luxurious cruises. She had grown bored with her snob-
bish husband and was not sorry he left her. She was traveling

the world to avoid him and for several days chose to sit at a table under Awad's supervision. He was attracted by her intermittent conversation, and she discovered him with an intellectual's discernment. One day she was puzzled and gazed at him intently, and said, "Impossible!"

"What do you mean?"

"For you to be here and nowhere else."

"I don't understand."

"I'm surprised, that's all."

"You mean I . . . ? But in my country they throw people like me in prison."

"That's terrible."

He smiled, and she smiled. She liked him. She extended her warm hand and said, "I'm pleased to meet you."

Before the end of the cruise, she had fastened onto him. "Awad, tell me about your country." They talked a great deal and had many conversations. They deadlocked at the drink of the south, however. She loved fine champagne, but tried to drink the pungent *arak* made from dates. First she tried a mouthful of it, and then a glass, then asked for more, and she was addicted. She pursued him, and he pursued her. She followed him wherever he went, and he traveled any distance to be near her. She was crazy about him, and he, the hater of slavery, enslaved her.

The years passed, but he had eyes for no one in the wide world but her. He forgot the whole past, his comrades, the south, his mother and uncle, Abdu Shindi, Demerdash, Rabi al-Salwawi, the officer Sirr al-Khatm; he was in a stupor from which he would never awaken. She loaned him books that affected him deeply. They read Tayib Saleh's *Season of the Migration to the North* together, but she did not sympathize with the hero, Mustafa Sa'id. She said he was just a sick, fanatical animal. After long hardship and effort on her part, he freed himself from the Dongola complex and the bowmen of the glance, the slaves of Nubia, and the Muslims' swords. She told him that history was just the dusty past and that to be obsessed with it just meant illness and death. What he had been was gone, and his dreams of a Nubian state were naïve, and just an injury of history.

"But we're still here," he protested. "We have our language and our own color."

"And in India and Russia there are countless ethnicities and languages."

She drew him closer into her tolerant thinking, and they became one body and one soul. She called him every day and waited for him in the ports, and she never grew impatient when her complicated divorce took time. She agreed with him that they would be married in the south, at the foot of the colossal statue at Abu Simbel—she had been active in the campaign to save it. Their wedding procession would be in a camel-borne litter, followed by dancers with swords and whips. A wedding party in Nubia, for a French woman, among his poverty-stricken people? How could that be? If she were to come in summer, she would try to flee after just an hour.

His mother paid no attention to his story. She had insisted, from the moment of his arrival, that he give her happiness by fulfilling half his faith—by marrying—and by renovating the house. He dodged the issue, procrastinated, and made excuses. Then he grew weary of her insistence; she would not leave him alone. So he told her his secret, despite the fact that he knew how deeply she hated the women of the north. He told her that Simone was from a faraway country and had nothing to do with her late husband's second wife, Ruhia; she was like one of the tourists she had seen in Aswan and the temples of Nubia. Hushia shrieked and beat her hands on her chest in terror: "*Hil-wa! Hil-wa!* Oh, no! Oh, poor Hushia! Oh, poor people, and your children! How can they pray? O God, my pain with Shalali and his son!"

"What's wrong, Mother?"

"This is a disgrace, Awad! A foreign woman, with a clitoris?"

"That's no problem, Mama, we'll circumcise her."

"Impossibie."

"Fine then, I won't get married at all."

"All my hopes come back to me, but in a way that's taboo!"

Taboo. The values of the south. When he was in Europe, he never asked anyone what their background was or about the ingredients of the food he was eating—he did not care whether it contained any pork, or kangaroo meat, or frog soup. He ate everything they ate and lived as they lived. What would his mother say if she knew that this French woman did not believe in religion at all—Simone had not even asked him about his beliefs, whether he was still a communist or had returned to Islam, or whether he had apostasized and gone back to his native paganism. These were marginal matters which they never discussed. She loved him, and he loved her, and that was enough. Whether they would marry in a church, or a mosque, or whether they had no official marriage at all—these were just details. They had met outside the borders of restrictions and obstacles. It was hard to convince his mother because she was from here, and believed in everything that was here: origin, religion, and ethnic community. And she would not give up her determination: "Early tomorrow morning I'm going to look for a bride for you."

"By God, Mother, leave it alone! You're giving me a headache!"

But she could not leave this subject alone or give his head a rest—she wanted to break it open to see what was inside it. She sought the help of the elders of the town, and they decided to hold a meeting to chastise and reform him.

4

There were few men left in the village. There were those who had held onto the useless land the government had given them, which they hopelessly tried to bring to life: the unemployable; the sick; those who had been crushed by the cities of the north, and returned almost mindless; teachers; those who had gone to work abroad and come home rich, but squandered it, gone broke, and traveled again. The cream of this group was now assembled as a council in Hushia al-Nur's house, to stand in unofficial judgment over Awad Shalali. At their head was the new mayor, Muhammad Hasan Khalil from the Miknab tribe. Awad Shalali tried to win them over with a pack of cigarettes, some expensive sweets, and a good dinner. They ate, drank, and smoked, and said prayers for their dead. They recited proverbs and sought comfort in verses from the Koran about how Paradise lay at the feet of mothers. They slowly made their way to the main topic. The old lady had summoned them, and they had to be fair to her. The mayor took the initiative with his subtlety and unflattering speech.

"You, sir. Why did you upset our patient lady?"

"Marriage is fate and destiny, sir."

"And where is your fate? You are like your father."

"Mr. Mayor, this is a question of taste, of inclination."

The mayor looked irritated and stood up. He lost his temper and began to attack Awad harshly:

"That is a philosophy of lies and doubletalk. Go ahead and say it—our girls aren't your type. Who do you think you are? Better than whom? Your only qualifications are a teaching credential and languages you learned in drawing rooms. Your brain has been pointing north your whole life. You were a respectable teacher, but you spurned God's blessings and lost yourself and worked in politics out of stupidity. In the end they imprisoned you, and then you ran away, abandoning your mother. Now you've come back wearing eyeglasses, with a forked tongue. Here we were saying, 'This boy has joined the British House of Commons!'—while you were clearing away customers' plates. You came back again to degrading jobs. What's wrong with our girls, effendi? Shall we throw them to the crocodiles in Lake Nasser? Or auction them off in slave markets? Listen to me, mister."

The mayor then mentioned the names of people from this or that village who had made it, or become rich and famous. "Haj Awadallah, a big boss in the sugar company, married his illiterate cousin. Bashir Abd al-Rahim, the director of the Bank al-Nilein in Khartoum, who did not forget the village that had begotten him and educated him. Abdu Shidayn, who had taught in France and been given a job by Hotels of Egypt, said, 'The girls of my country are the best.' Abu Zayd Awadallah, and others, a deputy cabinet minister, and another—a parliamentary deputy—and Ibrahim Idun, who has a managerial job. All of them held fast to their roots, because our girls are the most respectable in the world. You can leave one of them for years and she will keep your name and reputation safe—not like others, where a man goes away for two days and comes back to find another man on top of her. Look at your father and men like him. They abandoned their roots, and they were lost. Do you think the women of Cairo and foreign women love your blackness? If you were to go bankrupt, they'd throw you to the dogs in the street. But here, you get sick, you go broke, you get the mange, and she's by your side because she's your flesh and blood." The mayor concluded with a sigh and a question.

"So, you, sir—what's the real story with you?"

"The issue, Mr. Mayor, is—"

The mayor cut him off as if he had some score to settle. He stood up again and excitedly pounded the floor with his staff. The surrounding houses were silent as the women spied through their windows, awaiting the downfall of the renegade. The men let the mayor have the floor, because he was the best able to deal with gentlemen and educated people; he had been an employee of the elementary school before being pensioned off. He continued his attack as if he wanted to insult the Alyab now that he had taken the mayor's job away from one of them.

"The issue is what, sir? Do you think I'm some village idiot and you can shut me up with two words? I was one of the leaders of the Wafd Party before you were born. I understand politics very well. Who are you? Shall I tell the people, shall I tell Hushia who you are? Listen, you people of the Alyab, and you, too, Hushia. Your son was a communist. A communist means an atheist, and an atheist is someone who does not believe in God or His prophets. When they released him, he was so angry that he came to spread the good news of Dongola and the state of Nubia, and other such nonsense. He ruined the former mayor, and he ruined his mother, and abandoned her, and got Demerdash mixed up in it. Do you know, sir, where Demerdash is now? He believed your talk and imagined himself to be a Nubian leader, and he began to write petitions and brought a lawsuit against the government. It's been three years now and we have no idea where he is. Are you happy with your poor pupil? Sir, all our lives we have been cared for by Egypt and lived under its protection. And you come along at the end of time to try and drive a wedge between us and them and to start trouble. What would have happened if we had listened to you and they had bombed us with planes and wiped us out of existence? And come to think of it, where were you all this time? Did you ask yourself, even once, in your stupidity, like a mule, how your mother was living? Sir, your mother was on the brink of having to go and sit by the train tracks to beg for a living, and she would have, if it hadn't been for me and the people of this town. We decided to get her some charitable help. We fed and clothed her and took her to the doctor. Our daughters washed her clothes and served her. Do you understand why I don't like whores like you? And listen to the last thing I have to say. If you decide to travel again, take your mother with you. And no more nonsense. And to hell with you! You should be ashamed!"

Had the mayor gone too far and overstepped the bounds of good taste, or had he spoken rightly? The men averted their eyes in shame. They were not used to good deeds being made public, because southerners shared their last crumb with their needy neighbors. Hushia had wept the first day she accepted charity, but she had no choice after she had sold everything she had, and she had no idea where her son was. Awad Shalali felt parched, thirsty, and hot. This high-flown old Wafdist mayor, with his shrill voice, was another aspect of the things he hated, and which made him hate this country. He had defamed him, dragged his dignity in the dirt, and called him a whore. With two words he had erased his whole combatant history and turned him into a mere infidel, an angry fanatic for his people. But he had to stand up for himself. He had wronged his mother, wronged her terribly and unforgivably. His excuse was that his ties to his country had been cut and so he had only recently learned that his uncle had died bankrupt after a long illness, that his mother had gone blind, that the government had done nothing for her, and that everything had changed. He had learned all this only by chance, when he was getting drunk in a tavern in Athens, from one of his countrymen, who only then discovered that this was the southerner Awad Shalali, and that he had a mother and a nationality despite the Sudanese passport he carried. He had taken the first plane home. What strange years he had lived. He remembered Wahat and Bahr Jazuli, the official in Aswan. So deep was the abyss he inhabited that when he heard of the June "setback"—Egypt's defeat in the 1967 war—he gloated at the thought of those peacocks, and at the mere thought that this presaged the fall of military state.

Even the news of the more recent wars he heard apathetically. He felt no pride or happiness. It was like news of countries fighting in an unknown part of the world. But Simone read the newspapers eagerly.

"They've done something fantastic!" she said happily.

"Who?"

"Your people."

"My people?"

"They crossed the Canal."

"Oh."

"How can you say you are a loving person, when you heart is so full of that hatred?"

"What do you care whether they crossed the Canal or got drowned in it?"

"If you love, you forgive."

"And if you were wrongly imprisoned for ten years, you don't forget."

That night they stopped making love. The news of the terrible war going on in that faraway place had come between them. She spoke to him of tolerance and forgetting, and he described to her every day he had spent in Wahat. He told her that the prisons in the Middle East were not like the hotel-prisons of Europe. There, prisoners were turned into animals. There were no toilets or beds in the wards; there were only mats, bad food, usually two black potatoes, and hateful faces. The jailer was an ignorant peasant who made no distinction between prisoners and animals. He said. She said. She found him stubborn and vindictive and went away angry. They quarreled for two days. He tried to apologize and found her crying helplessly. She hugged him so tightly that she nearly broke his ribs, and said something strange.

"I feel like a failure."

"Failure?"

"There's a black spot in you I can't remove."

What a bizarre woman. How did she see him? Was he a laboratory rat to her? He left her and went home worried. He telephoned her the next day and told her about his mother and his wish to travel immediately. And she said something even stranger.

"Now you're on the road to recovery."

"Will you come with me?"

"I'll wait for you to come back. Give your mother my regards."

What recovery, what failure was she talking about? What was certain was that there was some misunderstanding between them. When he returned, he would find some way of reconciling with her. And his mother, whom he had forgotten all those years, did she have anything to do with this linguistic ambiguity? On the road to recovery. Did she see him as a sick man? Was he a sick man? His mother had suffered on his account for nineteen years. And Demerdash. Was he another victim? And the former mayor—had he paid a price for Awad's escape? If he had sent his mother the price of a single bottle of whiskey, she would have been able to live with her head held high. How had he given so much thought to his motherland and so little to his mother?

He had thought of repenting of his old mistakes and leaving her a large amount of money so she might hire a servant. Now he told them so, but they responded angrily.

"Do you think our daughters would work as servants for pay?"

"God forgive you, Awad!"

"Now we've heard everything."

"What kind of talk is that, effendi?"

"God help us!"

Haj Ahmad Abbas intervened and told them to be quiet. "Listen, people. Is it so bad, what he said? It was just a slip of the tongue. Now calm down."

When Ahmad Abbas spoke, they listened to him respectfully because he always found reasonable solutions and paid no mind to tribal sensitivities, to prejudice, or to chauvinism. The problem was now critical, so they let him take control of the situation, rather than the mayor, who was biased in favor of his tribe. Ahmad Abbas proposed a compromise: Awad Shalali would marry the Nubian girl of his choice and leave her to care for his mother when he traveled, if he so wished. Perhaps this marriage would bode well, and he would return to his senses.

"Well said, Haj."

"You are right, by God."

"Let him think about it."

"What do you think, Mayor?"

"It's this or disaster. Just as you say," he replied, preparing to leave.

Awad wanted to hire a servant. They were offering her for sale with a legal contract. He had no choice. Traveling with his mother was inconceivable. But to stay here at the government's mercy with the sword of the past over his head? It would be madness. The only solution was to flee like a coward on the first train, or perhaps to hold out a little, to deal with all the possibilities and try to find an honorable solution.

5

The mayor's words were poisoned arrows. His veiled threat had flexed his muscles and dug up forgotten history. He had meant what he said: obedience, or disaster. But he had told the truth, however shamefully. Had his mother really begged her bread while he was dining with Simone in the best restaurants in Paris? How had he forgotten her for so long? Tomorrow Simone would fall in love with someone else and kick him out the way she had kicked out her husband. She would go looking for a drink more exotic than arak. But his mother was right here, and she was the surviving symbol compensating for his failure to bring about justice and the dream of independent Nubia. His only option was to take Haj Ahmad Abbas's advice: a bride to serve her, who would cost him nothing but food, clothing, and his name, which she would share. These were wretched people who could not provide shelter for their own daughters. Otherwise, what was this explanation for such a strange marriage? It was a stay of execution, a primitive deal they were forcing him to accept.

"Yes, what do you want, Mother?"

"Only what God wants, my boy."

"What do you want me to do?"

"I want you to be happy, my boy."

"Your happiness is more important."

"I forgive you." She sighed. "You may travel, and stay away, and be safe, but visit every year, and send me letters, and let me know where you are. Bring the foreign woman when you come. Don't leave me at the mercy of these people. You heard with your own ears how they can be."

Hushia, with her heart of gold, had sensed his predicament and decided to give him his freedom, despite her cruel circumstances. After a moment, however, she changed her mind. If this crazy boy spread his wings and flew, he would never again come back to this nest. But if he married here, perhaps he would come back to settle here. Perhaps he would get homesick and come back. Perhaps he would have children. In any case, she could find someone companionable who would serve her. So she contradicted herself in her sad, quavering voice.

"No, my boy. Don't take me with you. Marry someone who can take care of me. I'm so tired, my boy. Sometimes I get thirsty, and there's no one to hand me the water jug. Sometimes I get up to walk, and I fall down, and I call out for people, and not a soul hears me. Sometimes I go to bed ill, without any food or medicine. What would I have done without Halima, may God reward her! People have changed, my boy, in this terrible place here. What's it called? Silsilah Mountain—Chain Mountain! It's a chain around our necks. In our old land, if you sighed, your neighbor would ask you right away what the problem was. They shared food. If you were blind, they'd take your hand and lead you to where you needed to go, even if it was at the end of the earth. We sat with the sick and suffering until they were cured. But here, my boy, where are those people? I can't go on any more. I don't have a daughter or a sister. Swear by the Prophet that you'll help me before you leave."

Hushia wept, and Awad Shalali bled; he felt tortured and torn. The images passed before his eyes with infinite cruelty: a blind old woman, alone, in a lonely house. She fell, and her blood spilled. She could die and rot before anyone found her. And this woman was his mother, and he could not possibly leave her. If he did that, he would be one of the most despicable people.

"Then that's it," he told her, meaning what he said. "I will not leave."

"What about your work?"

"You are my work and my only concern."

"Don't bother with me, my boy."

"You are all I care about."

"Marry and then leave."

"I'll do whatever you want."

"So go visit the family of your bride."

"Who do you mean, Mother?"

"Halima, our neighbor. She's from our tribe."

Hushia al-Nur trilled with joy and sang, and the village sang with her. The mayor's ire faded because this was the worst renegade, the chief rebel, and he was being tamed. If he got away from them, all the young men would do as he did, and the number of unmarried girls would climb even higher. Awad Shalali felt very sorry for himself. The sheikh and the best man—the deputy victim—the joyous trilling and the southern songs: *"This boy's hair is curly—our bridegroom is a happy man!"* They wound their way through all the streets of the village. He remembered Abdu Shindi and felt sad. This kind of primitive celebration was the kind of thing Simone dreamed of. They led the procession with volleys of rifle shots, and all the young men stood outside the house, under the newlyweds' window. They shouted and made mocking remarks as they always did and teased the bridegroom with ribald words of encouragement.

6

They were two strangers confined in a suffocatingly hot room. It was an inhuman heat; the very walls and ceiling throbbed with fiery heat. There was no door or window. Every corner of this cell was aromatic with musk, sandalwood, strong perfumes, and Sudanese incense, and ornamented with palm branches. A platter of pigeon stuffed with roasted green wheat was the newlyweds' supper. In this lethal heat it was impossible to converse; their souls wanted to part from their bodies. Silence. He waited. Unease and surprise. A stranger. Waiting. The night was slipping away from them. In the morning they would have to delight their elderly families. Awad Shalali took off his clothes, leaving on only his elegant Parisian underpants, as if he were on a beach. But there was no beach; this was a hellish desert land that reached into the depths of one's soul. His head ran with boiling sweat. Halima the bride was fortified inside her thick clothing and veil. She did not say a word; it was as if she were mute. She would not move her lips until she had experienced the sweetness of hearing him talk, as was the custom. He told her, "Why don't you take your clothes off," so that she might be free of those before they suffocated her. He meant no more than that, but she recoiled and curled up like a hedgehog, thinking that the battle had begun. What could make him desire a miserable creature curled up in an oven, except air? And where was the air? He shouted, puffing, "Air! Air!" She hurried over to him with a small, hand-worked fan and sat silently beside him, fanning him. He smiled despite his misery: the prince and his slave. He remembered Simone, and Husna the daughter of

Mahmoud Mustafa Sa'id, the heroes of *Season of the Migration to the North*. He was surprised at Mustafa's ability to adapt to the climate of the south after he had lived so long in the civilization of the West. Now he had to make love and have sex with a woman who was a stranger to him, a woman he was now seeing for the first time. He knew that she was only an instrument with which he could win his freedom. It was an unjust solution, and he was burned by the fire of injustice. Should he leave her a virgin or tell her the truth about the details of the bargain? Would this night end peacefully? Yes, he knew she had served his mother for years, hoping for a reward. He was not God, to reward people. The world was fire, and here in front of him was a woman on the night of her life, and he had a heavy duty which he could not fulfill. He had asked for air, not sex. The tradition was that he ought to take her against her will, like the knights of dusty, bygone ages. He drank a glass of arak, and fire upon fire settled in his stomach. He turned on the news of the world and paused when he heard dance music. He stood up and staggered drunkenly; she watched him stealthily and smiled. He offered her the glass, but she pushed his hand away.

"God forbid."

"This is made from dates."

"May God guide you!"

He got drunker and looked around. In this room he saw her: brown skin and shiny teeth. She was smiling. He was her legitimate husband according to the faith of this land. Was there anything else? His problem lay in starting—how might he begin to talk to her, to start a conversation that would bring them to intimacy and understanding? She must have sensed his unease and discomfort because she earnestly offered him the platter of pigeon.

"Eat and enjoy."

It was a good start, even though she made the wrong choice, tempting his stomach. He had to help her. "How are you?" he asked kindly. "I am very well," she said. "How are you?" He replied, "I'm fine, but hot." She moved closer and fanned him rapidly. He felt her warm breath and stroked her cheek gently. She moved away. Feeling the effects of the liquor, he got up and went after her. The bad liquor had given him courage. He jumped behind her and grabbed her veil and braids. She bit him lightly and slipped away, and she ran around the room again. He stayed behind her, and some objects broke. Her ornaments fell, one after the other. Hushia must be listening because he heard trilling. He was tired and gave up.

"So, Halima?"

If he left her a virgin and just went away traveling, the rumors would spread that he had rejected the marriage because he was weak. Halima moved away, rubbed her palms together, to anger him. This adventure represented her whole future, and when they recalled their wedding night together, she would taunt him with his failure. Here, being a man meant power: crudity, a mustache, a voice, a stick. There, in Europe, even a fallen woman could choose whom she would marry, and choose him among any number of others. He had to follow the rules of the country in which he found himself. He did not want her, and she had not chosen him. Her father had sold her, and his mother had bought her. The religion sanctioned it, and the deal was made. Awad had another drink, and when he saw her standing there, as if challenging him, he became an animal. He attacked her and bent her arm back. She could not move. He pulled her violently to him, which is what she had been hoping for. She gave in happily, not knowing the secrets of this marriage. They told women, "Congratulations! Justice is yours!" and the women had to nod in agreement. All they cared about was that the bridegroom be a southerner who had money to spend—old or young, demented or sane, what did they care? Awad Shalali was the ideal of every southern woman, but he was a fleeting bridegroom—nothing could make him stay here. There was a shriek of pain from these strangers' room, then a rifle shot and joyful trilling. She felt a happiness she had never known before, never since she was born.

"You're a naughty man," she told him.

"You're sweet," he told her.

In the end, the demons of liquor and mischief had contrived a unique night for her, with an experienced man, a night such as she had dreamed of for months and years.

7

The sky aimed its volcano-like eruptions of fire at the whole south. The temperature crept toward 125 degrees, to everyone's surprise. At twelve noon, the land was Hell itself: the sand burned like fire, the water boiled in the faucets, and people's throats were utterly parched. They sought relief from the agony in the hot shade, but there was no relief. The only hope was that the sun would go down and never rise again during the summer months. Their imploring hands were lifted up toward the sky seeking help, but there was no help, because the sun had determined to burn them alive. For in this land, they both blamed and adored the sun, for there was cold, ice, and night that lasted half the year. There had to be some balance in this lopsided world: eternal spring and justice were mere dreams. Awad Shalali could not adapt to the southern climate, with its sun, restrictions, and stubborn traditions. He was even now preparing to travel to the land of the free, and no one could blame him, because he had secured his mother's future with money and a legal servant. If he told Simone the details of this bizarre visit, just as they had happened, what would she say? He had only the remotest hope that she would take all his explanations seriously; he would have to tell some white lies. He would tell her that they had forced him to marry, or shut him up in a pharaonic-era cave until the wedding night until he signed the contract, with the Koran and swords held over his head, that it was just a sham marriage because he had slept in a separate room. Would she believe him? He thought not. He had told her the smallest details of his childhood, and she knew from all he told her that the Nubians were peaceful people. They did not carry rifles, swords, or clubs. If they had stood up for themselves, the northerners would never have been able to build the first reservoir and the second dam—not without bloody resistance. The Upper Egyptians carried rifles, and the Basharis carried swords and daggers. And so her information went beyond the temples of Abu Simbel, Kalabshah, the straits, and ancient history in vanished kingdoms. It would be best not to say anything to her, because she would never share him with another. She—like the women of her country—was not familiar with unstable emotions. When she grew bored with her husband, she got rid of him. There, they separated easily when normal marital relations became impossible.

Here, obedience was the rule. Halima used every feminine trick to foil his plans to escape. She cast a spell. She made herself beautiful. She gave herself to him with a generosity unknown to girls here. She begged and pleaded, and then begged and pleaded with Hushia, and with her father. She pretended to be ill, and then she cried and threatened. The poor young woman did not know that she represented his one chance to leave, not to stay.

"By God, don't go."

"I have to make a living, Halima."

"You don't have to travel."

"Everyone travels, Halima."

"But they come back."

"I will, too."

"Swear!"

"I swear to God, I'll come back."

"Swear by the Koran."

"Believe me!"

"There must be some other woman who's put a spell on you."

"Don't be crazy."

"So, why are you in such a hurry to leave?"

"Look, girl, I have a job and responsibilities!"

She did not believe a word of it. She had a recurrent nightmare that he would never return. She collapsed when everyone was seeing him off at the station. She sat in a heap, holding her head, which ached with thinking, and her tears never stopped flowing.

"Goodbye, my boy!"

"Goodbye."

Halima trudged home shattered. She entered the house, and it seemed desolate and empty. "This son of yours," she said dazedly to Hushia al-Nur, "he's strange. He didn't cry one tear, and he didn't tell me goodbye. He was happy to go. That was the first time I've ever seen anyone happy to leave. I wish I knew why!" This was the truth. Awad Shalali's heart was dancing with happiness as the train moved and then chugged out of Kalabshah Station. He looked out of the window and saw the well-wishers and the whole village, and they seemed to be ghosts, like a short film running through his memory: Demerdash screaming at him, wearing the uniform of a northern prison: "*You coward! You coward!*" And Abdu Shindi, wherever he was, in a hospice, or the lunatic asylum in al-Abassia, singing "*My land, my homeland.*" His mother, who had lost her sight, had nothing more to lose but her life. Halima was now a means to salvation. The crowd of faces, his uncle, Abbas Tawfiq, the mayor, Sergeant Sirr al-Khatm, Bahr Jazuli, and the doctor. They were angry with him, and his comrades in the Café Riche in Cairo were probably making insinuations against him. But why? *The hellish sun disk is behind me now.* He thought of Husna the daughter of Mahmoud, and Mustafa Sa'id; Wahat; he thought of all this, and felt nothing special or meaningful at all. These were only events and names that occupied a humble corner of his skull. He closed his eyes and summoned up Simone's happy face.

PART THREE

The Sorrows of Hushia and Halima

1

Halima waited and her waiting grew long because she was like the other forsaken women of Nubia, all of whom were waiting for men who had journeyed far away, to the cities of Egypt, the Arab lands, and overseas. They lost track of time; they got lost in its tracklessness and were dazzled by its passage. Then they caught themselves and regained their awareness of it. For he who made money came home triumphant. He who found work would settle in the land of Egypt and dwell there and summon his wife to join him. He who was crushed started over. All of them had addresses in well-known places and corresponded with their families, and the letters were almost as good as seeing them again. But Halima's marriage, and her wait, were unrivaled. She counted the days and then the months. A year passed like a whole lifetime. This absentee had a heart of stone: he had sent only one letter since his departure. He gave no word of a visit. He did not give them his address. Hushia al-Nur prayed for his success, health, and prosperity, and Halima prayed for him. They thought of him as living at sea; but did not the sea have shores and ports? This was a man without a home port. Where could he be? Her married life had lasted less than a month. Her misfortune was that she loved him. Life without him was empty. What kind of marriage was this? She had gone from being her father's wife's servant to being the servant of this bossy, senile old woman. Before her marriage, she had served and helped her because they were relatives and neighbors, and the old woman thanked her and prayed for her. Now, she gave orders. Was Halima not the servant she had personally selected?

"I want to eat, Halima."

"Yes, ma'am."

"I want a drink."

"Yes, ma'am."

"Help me up."

"Yes, ma'am."

Her demands never stopped. Day and night, she asked, "Take me to the doctor in the clinic." "I'm hot—fan me." "Bolt the door, Halima." "Who was that knocking just now, Halima?" "Where are you going?" "Who are you talking to?" "Halima! Halima!" She was a servant, a nurse, a companion, an escort, a slave. If she were slow to respond, Hushia scolded her. If she behaved nicely, Hushia suspected something. If she wanted to go out, Hushia prevented her. She got so upset with Hushia, and with herself, that she cursed her, screamed at her, tore her clothes, and nearly burned herself with gas. Then she gathered her clothes and went back to her father's house, swearing she would not return to Hushia's house until her husband came back and restored her freedom with a divorce. But when she turned to her father to take her side, he gave her advice and scolded her.

"You get good luck and you throw it away, bint Shaya!" they said. Shaya was her mother's name.

"My conscience is clear."

"You left Hushia all alone?"

"Good riddance to her."

"What are people saying?"

"You married me off to a man, not to Hushia al-Nur and 'people.'"

"For God's sake, what's your problem? Do you have money?"

"Plenty of money."

"Did Hushia prevent you from spending it?"

"No, never."

"Is she miserly?"

"No."

"So what's the problem?"

"I was fed up—I was ready to die."

"I'll kill you myself, you little slut. A divorce will get you nowhere but back home."

Halima returned, defeated, broken, and reluctant, to find that Hushia had become even more unreasonable and bossy. She harassed and humiliated her with trivial demands which were impossible and unfriendly. Halima was bewildered. She did not know where to turn. Her father was stupid, her husband was a tyrant, and no one understood her plight or the plight of all women in this land of waiting.

2

Women. Women. Wherever she went, they were all she saw, crowding into the markets, streets, parties, funerals, the telephone and telegraph office, the railroad station, at the public water spigot and sitting on benches, tense and argumentative, quarrelsome, and always shouting.

At night, their suffering began with the slow passage of

time, their frustrated desires, and their passion for their absent
men. The fiery climate kindled their own heat, and they did not
know how to overcome it except by beseeching God to keep
Satan at bay, and praying for patience, patience, patience. Halima,
like the other young, abandoned wives, was pursued by men,
but few lost their modesty. Hamad Tawfiq, the most shameless
man, was behind the murder of a virgin and the divorce of a
married lady, and he was still able to corrupt. The Tawfiq clan
was from the Alyab tribe; one of them was the senior watchman
and aspired to be mayor and the other was a wolf. The shame
was reserved for women—the men were never blamed. Halima
was Hamad's anticipated next prey. His experience made him
understand the precariousness of her delicate, difficult position;
he put her under surveillance. He watched her. He flirted with
her; he was always behind her or in front of her. He was wherever she was. She warned him and cursed him and changed her
schedule, going out at different times. She stopped going to her
usual places. However, he remained patient. Halima knew how
insolent and debauched he was; if she had words with him or
forcibly repelled him, he would find a way of smearing her reputation with false rumors, as he had done with other women. She
exchanged a hopeful look with him, and a smile of fear. She
pleaded with her eyes for him to leave her alone, but this devil
was a nightmare who would not go away. Between a restless
night of heat, gnats, and unsettling dreams, and a day that would
not end, and the control of that tyrannical old woman, Halima
was enduring terrible bitterness, until she received a letter which
saved her from imminent madness and changed her utterly. She
called on Haj Ahmad Abbas and showed him the letter for the
second time. She knew its contents but wanted more.

"Again, Halima?" asked Ahmad Abbas testily.

"I want to understand perfectly."

"It's just a letter, Halima. Whatever you say. I understand."

Ahmad Abbas, custodian of all the village's secrets, marveled at Halima's infatuation with this ordinary paper letter. Dozens of expatriates send these exhortations to patience. "*I will be coming, God willing, early next year. I'm sending you the money you need to repair and enlarge the fountain, and to install water and electricity, to buy a refrigerator, a ceiling fan, and an air conditioner. I may bring visitors with me. I hope my friend your father will help you with the problems you are having. In closing, greetings to my mother, Halima, Abbas Tawfiq, and Haj Ahmad Abbas, and all the people of the village, lest I forget any by name. I hope you will let me know whether Demerdash has been released or not. And special greetings to the reader of this letter*. Did you understand?"

"He said greetings to Halima."

"It is the same letter, in your name, my girl."

"So, he said, 'Greetings to Halima.'"

"Yes, by Almighty God, he did."

"Good. So, early in the year means when?"

"Early in the year, Halima."

"How many days from now? How many months?"

"God knows."

"What's his address?"

"There is no address. It's just a postal letter with the seal of the foreign country."

"What visitors?"

"People, Halima, human beings."

"He means men?"

"And maybe women."

"God forbid."

"Halima, God's book says a man may have two wives or even four."

"You men always say what suits you best."

"God forgive you!"

"Who's with you there, Halima?" called Hushia al-Nur, whose sharp hearing had picked up their voices.

"It's me, Hushia."

"Very good, Haj."

"All is well."

"Please, Haj, I want to talk to you."

Ahmad Abbas murmured the formula *In the name of God, the Compassionate, the Merciful,* and entered. He leaned over, despite his old age, to kiss Hushia's hand, and she wished him health and well-being and moved her head close to his.

"There's something strange in that letter, Haj."

He waited for her to explain. He did not know what there was in this letter, written in plain Arabic, that so pained these two crazy women.

"Has he done it and married the foreign woman, I wonder?" Hushia asked with profound sadness.

"Foreign woman?"

"Lower your voice, Haj."

"What are you talking about, Hushia?"

"Oh, Haj, you don't know this boy."

Halima entered soundlessly, with tea. She wanted to know the secret or surprise of the complaining old woman, but she did not pay attention to what they were saying. It was enough for Awad Shalali to come, even if a thousand women came with him. This time he would not get away from her. She would seek out the assistance of the most skillful sorceress of the whole south. She would have such a powerful spell cast on him that even the blue devil would never be able to break it.

3

By January first, three years after Awad Shalali had left, she had received no further letter nor any telegram giving the date of his arrival, and yet she waited for him, as if his arrival were a certainty. The temperature of her readiness rose. She incensed the house and perfumed the water jug, swept the whole house, and prepared some fowl and sacrificial animals. She dyed herself with henna, put on perfume, and dressed in her most expensive silk, so that she looked like a fabulous bride. She got to the station before everyone else, with a tray of popcorn and dates. A question ran through the village: Who was Halima waiting for? Hushia al-Nur thought this over in her mistrustful mind, and thought, *God help us.* Everyone had the same thought, and questioned her sanity. Otherwise, what could explain all this fevered activity to meet a man who was still far away? The train had whistled and arrived, let off its passengers, and taken its dreams on to Aswan, and Halima still stood there dazed, until a woman spoke to her.

"The train is gone, Halima."

"Train?"

"He'll arrive safe and sound tomorrow."

"Tomorrow?"

"God give you patience."

"Patience?"

She left the station in despair, utterly shattered, and went to the telegraph office.

"Yazid Effendi, is there any news?"

"Bless you, Cousin."

"Any telegram from the man?"

"Who's the man?"

"The effendi, Hushia's son."

"What, aren't I the only man?"

"All you do is joke."

"You should greet me first, Halima."

"I swear by the Prophet's tomb, you are stupid."

"It is a duty to greet people, by God."

His hand, offered through the little window, was an open invitation to friendship and innocent affection, but his welcom-

ing smile did not hide predator's fangs like those of Hamad
Tawfiq. He was just a shy teenager. She was not afraid of him,
even though he was one of her pursuers, because his amorous
efforts never made it farther than the telegraph office. But a question perplexed her: did he do this with all the women who came
in here, or was she the only one? Whatever the case, she would
never respond to his overtures while she was married to another
man. He might be the one she wanted, though, if she became
free through a divorce. There was nothing wrong with keeping
him ready for the day he was needed. She smiled and gave him
her hand. He clasped it between his two hot, trembling palms.
She loved his heat, and her body quivered slightly. She felt uncom-
fortable and withdrew her hand. She left, adjusting her clothing.
She almost fell; her heart pounded with joy and fear.

4

The first month of that third year passed, and still there
was no news. Halima changed; she was like a madwoman. Neither
day nor night brought her comfort. She yearned for a letter or a
telegram. She lived for the whistle of the passing train, the sound
of car horns, and even the buzz of an airplane. Any knock at the
door made her jump up and rush to it. She rejoiced at the sound
of any voice calling out. She waited and waited, but the waiting was destructive and would wear out even the strongest
nerves.

"Patience, Halima."

"Why doesn't he send any news?"

"Patience, my girl."

"Why doesn't he at least tell us what his excuse is?"

"I said, patience."

"Your son is a liar, Hushia."

Halima had become the talk of the gossipy old women of

the village, as well as of the lustful young men and busybodies. She came and went, sat down, talked, got dressed, all as usual, but if she went to the station, they said, "She's lost her mind." If she stopped to talk with a man, they said, "She's a slut." Once, they saw her running after a returning emigrant, calling, "Awad! Awad Shalali!" The poor woman was a shadow of herself as she made the daily rounds of her triangle of hope—the telegraph, the station, and the post office—before returning to the sorrowful place where she sat by the wall. This was the same place where Hushia al-Nur had lost her eyesight. The rumor was that an envious woman had invoked the evil eye on her because of all the glory she enjoyed: the electricity, her fan, the repairs to her house, and all the money she was able to spend. How many southern women delighted in this? One hostile old woman said, "We've lived and seen all the women on earth—tell me by God, people, is there anything she doesn't have?" Even her father threatened to beat or even kill her.

"Enough scandals, Halima!" he told her.

"What have I done?"

"Stay inside your house."

"I can't stand that old owl's house!"

"Come to your senses, bint Shaya!"

"Yes, my mother was Shaya, the one you killed with your cruelty."

"Your mother was crazy like you."

"God bless your sanity."

"I'll break your neck."

"At least then I'd be rid of you."

He ran after her with a sickle, cursing her mother, the midwife who had presided at her birth, and the bridal assistant who had circumcised her. Some people got between them. Halima did not care whether she lived or died. She went to the telegraph office, and asked Yazid Abd al-Wahab to write her a telegram to her husband.

"What's his address?" asked Yazid in surprise.

"A foreign country."

He laughed at her stupidity and spoke sweetly to calm her down. "Forget foreign places. Let's stay here at home."

"How can you say that to me, effendi?"

"It's the truth, by God."

"What's wrong with you, man? You've lost your mind."

"I don't sleep at night."

Then he sang a bit of a southern song: "At night I don't *sleep, I count the stars*." She left him singing, running away, but wished she could be near him, to tell him her troubles. Was it fair that it had been her lot to get the absent traveler, instead of this southerner who stayed put? At the corner, Hamad Othman stood, waiting, singing the eternal song of Nubia: "*Brown skin, O brown skin!*" She spat at him and hurried into the house, slammed the door, and dropped to the floor, weeping.

5

The third year of waiting was half over. The mailman came to her out of breath, running with excitement. "Good news, Halima! A registered letter, Halima!" She gave him the biggest tip in the history of Nubia and made him stay to read the precious letter. She did not have the time or patience to go and get the master of all secrets, Haj Ahmad Abbas.

"Are you paying attention, Halima?"

"Keep reading."

"Should I read it again?"

"That's enough."

A few dry lines. A fatal letter from an accursed husband. She was thunderstruck and shattered. She collapsed to cry and almost screamed. The world spun around her.

"Get cologne, someone! She's dizzy!"

"Make her drink water."

She came to and was fully conscious. She apologized, and the faces around her seemed hideous; they were the disgusting faces of heartless men, of a village that deserved to be burned down. A man for whom one waited so long excused himself from coming because of a sudden pain he had, but he promised he would come in the future. He enjoined her to take care of his mother, thanked her, and enclosed a check for more money than usual. His mother and money. But for her, Halima, the wife— not a word. The only good thing about this letter was its return address. At last the crocodile had stepped onto land. Now she could write to him. What would she tell him? Would she demand her legal rights? Before, he had neglected his mother for nine years, and she was his next victim. He would not respond, no matter how she begged. Her only alternative was to request a divorce. She went to her father weeping, the letter in her hand, and got the answer she expected.

"Money! He sent more than usual."

"Yes."

"And you have a better house than the mayor."

"True."

"You have silk and gold."

"Thank God."

"You eat the best foods."

"You don't understand women."

"What do you mean, bint Shaya?"

"We aren't oxen, that turn a water wheel, and eat grass, and lie down to sleep!"

"What else?"

"You've all tricked me, but you're brainless."

"Another word, and I'll cut your tongue out."

"You're always cutting out tongues or cutting off heads. You have no morals."

"Shut up, you slut."

He lunged at her with all his weight and knelt on her. She slapped him, and he bit her and put his hand around her neck. His wife screamed, and the rest of the women shouted and grabbed him. Halima escaped and ran to the telegraph office, intent upon the decision she had made. She would not give it up. It would be a slap at the law all men lived by and at the traditions of the south. She stood before the telegraph office employee, her decision steadfast.

"You've kept our secret, Yazid Abd al-Wahab?"

"Not a soul knows, Halima."

"No one knows?"

"Don't worry."

Yazid Effendi's imagination ran wild; he made his own guesses and had his own expectations, and went beyond barriers and restrictions. He had seen dogs on top of one another, and thought of the weddings he had seen and the filthy stories he had heard from the returning emigrants about women and night-time encounters, and what they called red nights. He imagined himself with Halima, situations and positions. Her commanding voice brought him back.

"Write, effendi."

Write what? This was bad news, Yazid. Some other man was involved here. He was always joking, but nothing had happened between them; all they had done was hold hands and laugh. Nothing was wrong with that. His lips trembled uncontrollably as he asked, frightened, "What should I write?"

"A telegram to this man. I have his address."

Yazid sighed with relief. He caught his breath.

"What do you want to say?"

"Three words."

"What are they?"

"Come, or send for me, or—or—"

"Or what?"

"Or divorce me."

Yazid stopped writing and put down his pen. He gazed at her for a long time. This was the first time, since he had started working in the telegraph office, that a Nubian woman had asked for a divorce in a telegram. If he obeyed her, the blame would fall on him. He was a member of her tribe. Would he go back on his promise? He heard Halima telling him to hurry.

"Have you written it?"

"What does your father say?"

"I have no father or mother. Write it or I'll go to Kom Ombo and send it from there."

"What about after the divorce?"

"God will look after me."

"All right. Put your thumbprint here."

Yazid turned the dial of his small radio and it emitted a tender northern song, expressing, by coincidence, a sad event: *"It has to be one way or the other: take me, or I'll come to you."*

"Are you listening, Halima?"

"God take you all."

"All of us?"

"There isn't one respectable man among all you Alyab."

"God forgive you."

"That's what I think."

"Let's talk about it."

"God damn you to Hell with the rest of them."

Her sharp tongue did not express what was in her heart. She was not serious in resisting or cursing him; sometimes in the south, a curse expressed love or friendship, and even throwing a stone was like exchanging flowers. If she counted the times she had visited the telegraph office, she would have realized what her true feelings were. But the tragedy of hearts in this country was that there was no rational accounting. When Halima turned around and left, she gave him a smile of apology even as she dreamed of him as a husband who would fill her house and every day of her life with his friendly voice and company. She

wanted him because he was not ugly or a wolf like Hamad
Tawfiq, who had followed her now and actually blocked her
path. She tried to avoid him, but he tricked her. She bent to the
ground and grabbed a handful of earth which she threw at his
white clothing.

"Damn you! You dirty man!"

He answered in kind: "You're Yazid's bitch!"

She confronted him angrily.

"Go to hell, you piece of trash!"

"I can expose you."

"Expose what? You're the pervert, all you Wahbab!"

Tribes, towns, and scandals. The Wahbab were a branch of
the Alyab. She heard him threaten her. She hated them. It was a
man's world. Everything was in their favor. They gave the
orders and women had to obey. She stood in front of the house
but did not go in. She felt depression and repulsion at this place
and its people. Hushia sat like a princess, smoking her pipe and
demanding whatever she wanted. Halima could not believe that
this Hushia had not gone near a man except during two months
of her whole life. Was she some kind of prophetess or saint?
Had she been afflicted when she sent the telegram to her husband? And what was the expected reply? What would people
say about her? Sitting in her sorrow, she heard the warm voice
of an Upper Egyptian worker, singing to his faraway love: "*I
have received no letter. Time, you are a traitor—what have you
done with my love? Time, you are a traitor.*" He repeated the
same verse many times. His name was Maadul, and he was the
Upper Egyptian who wandered through these villages with the
southern contractor to renovate and whitewash houses and to
enlarge the guest rooms. All the expatriates renovated their
houses and added tiling and roofs to their open courtyards. She
had contracted with the carpenter a week ago to make some
improvements that Hushia insisted upon. This Upper Egyptian
guarded the lumber and supplies at night and worked digging in

the soil and sand during the day. She had never noticed him the way she would notice another human being who had his own existence and could sing or move his listeners by singing, "I have received no letter." She wondered who he was singing to. She was drawn to his beautiful, tender voice, which made her feel lonely. Two tears ran from her eyes. Her body shook with emotion; she wished this song would last forever.

6

It was the hellish August of the south, the most terrible month of the year. No breeze stirred to blow the affliction away, and no sleep descended to relieve weary eyes. The ceiling fans shifted the dust. The sun roasted them by day, and the heat suffocated them by night. Where was their refuge? When would deliverance come? Halima and Hushia lay on beds side by side in the middle of the open courtyard, trying to escape from the oven-like indoor rooms.

Halima tossed and turned like a fish just pulled from the water. She fanned the edge of her nightgown to try and move the air. This land was hell, and its women were abandoned. The days had passed, yet she received no reply to her telegram, so she sent another. Still there was no reply. She began to doubt that the address was the correct one. And no matter what people swore to her, she would never believe that Hushia had stayed away from men her whole life, because there was no such thing as a woman prophet. Even prophethood was an honor for men only! Halima's night was unending. If she dozed off for a second, she was overtaken by obscene dreams in which she saw naked men sharing her: Hamad Tawfiq, Yazid Abd al-Wahab, the mayor, Ahmad Abbas, and even her father, while Awad Shalali, bizarrely, stood nearby, giving encouragement, telling the men what to do, and applauding. But Maadul the Upper

Egyptian saved her. He hit them on the head with his heavy club and protected her with his unrolled turban. He carried her away in his strong arms, and she hugged him and clung to him, then awoke in terror from her brief slumber, drenched with sweat and ashamed of herself. She asked God to forgive her and said two prayers, though it was not prayer time. Where was dawn, with its light, to chase away the satanic darkness? Where was the air? Where was Awad Shalali?

Between sleep and wakefulness, Hushia murmured:

"Bolt the door, Halima."

"I left it open."

That was a provocative answer. It was an invitation to the argument, which she wanted and would bring about intentionally. It was a necessary attempt to escape from the predicament of this solitude, silence, and the tricks of demons. Yes, there had to be an argument, and noise, and screams. Hushia al-Nur must have been sleeping or dreaming of doors and bolts, or perhaps she decided that night was not the time for a battle, but she was still talking.

"I want a drink, Halima."

"Get up and get a drink."

"My throat is dry, my girl."

"You have the refrigerator and the water jug."

"Get me a drink, God keep you."

"Protect me or abandon me, who cares."

There was going to be a battle. Why was everyone sleeping comfortably when she was on the verge of madness? Hushia had swallowed the insult and was silent. This crabby, troublesome, crooked old woman had plotted against her and denied her a chance to escape. She should scream now about something that hadn't happened—that a scorpion had stung her or a thief had broken in. Or that a demon had frightened her. Anything. This hot night would not pass peacefully—there must be some catastrophe so that future generations would remember her. Should she scream out that Awad Shalali was dead, and then receive condolences? Should she set the village on fire and burn everyone alive? This night was hell. There was fire in the earth and in people's souls, and a savage desire, beyond human endurance, was burning her body. Maadul the Upper Egyptian was awake, singing, as usual. The contractor had told her that their work here was finished; tomorrow both he and the Upper Egyptian would move on to another house, perhaps in some far-off village, and she would have no sweet voice to soothe her loneliness. The night was long. She closed her eyes a little and was prey again to filthy dreams. She saw Awad Shalali naked, with dozens of blonde women, who passed him along, ecstatically and forcefully. She stretched out her hand to save him, but they grabbed her and tried to tear her with their long fingernails. Yet again, only the Upper Egyptian saved her at the last moment, while all the men of the village watched and gloated. She got up. All her calm and sleep were gone. She drank some cold water, prayed, and spent a while reciting the Verse of the Throne several times. But her affliction was more powerful than prayers and Koranic verses. She needed Awad Shalali. Now. He was a strange man who talked even more strangely. He was all secrets. She never once saw him pray or recite the Koran; he never said "In the name of God, the Compassionate, the Merciful" before eating, and never thanked God when he had finished. She did not know why he had been imprisoned for ten years. And why had he disappeared for nine years? Once she heard him raving about Demerdash. What was between these two men? Once when Awad was drunk, he said, "Farewell, Dongola." Shyly Halima asked him, "Who is Dongola? Is it that woman's name?" He said, "Stupid! Dongola is a city in Sudan. The people there speak our language, and in ancient times, it was the capital of Lower Nubia. Nubia had a ruler, and knights, and learning, and it was independent. Now do you know what Dongola is?" She remembered the very black men who cut three long slits on their faces.

One of them was named Dongolawi, and they lived in the far south. Why would he dream of them?

"Did you understand?" he asked.

"Your other wife is named Dongola."

He laughed all day long, and whenever they sat together or talked, he would say, "Stupid. There isn't a lady in this world named Dongola." She was sure this was her name. The heat was unbearable. This night was a nightmare in real life. Time stopped in one moment; it did not budge forward or backward. Hushia's snoring upset her—it grated on her nerves. How were the women of Nubia now? Were they as tormented as she was? The Upper Egyptian was singing: "*I am thirsty, maidens!*" She was thirsty enough to die—how could she quench it? Tomorrow night, she would not be hearing him. So this night was goodbye? His beautiful voice was her only comfort in this conspiratorial silence. Mercy, Lord. What torture, to wait more than thirty months, with dozens of women standing around pointing at her? Surely this Upper Egyptian was singing to her, to draw her attention to him. He was the only man in this lonely night. She would strike a blow where no one expected it. She would insult them as they had insulted her. He was a non-person; all his time was dedicated to work and the drink of water he was asking for so kindly. He was just a few steps away, because strangers, especially foreign workers, did not enter the houses of the village. Someone like this grimy, dirty, rough Upper Egyptian, who almost never bathed, would be the last to think of a southern woman—if he thought at all. His first and only consideration was to feed himself, and he had no sufferings like those of Halima or other women. This was a luxury unavailable to him, but tonight he was Halima's dream, and her chosen method was to destroy her people and to wreak vengeance on them. All that was needed was the courage of a knight. She would open the door to him, and he would attack her and take her by force, and she would give him the opportunity by pretending to be asleep.

"Hushia. Hushia al-Nur. You bitch."

There was no sound and no echo. She was fast asleep. There was only Halima and the devils. For the third time she prayed, she knew not for how long, but the fire did not go out. Awad Shalali did not come and Hushia al-Nur did not get up, and daybreak did not come. It was a triple conspiracy. Like a woman lost or drugged, she got up. She put on perfume, unbraided her hair, and put on her satin. She opened the courtyard door and went back to bed, where she waited in a flirtatious pose. She waited. And still waited. The stupid son of a bitch was still singing. The coward. She went to the door and called out in a whisper, "You! Pssst! Pssst!" Nothing. She waited. He did not come; he was not going to come. She went into the kitchen and carried out the leftover chicken and bread and a bottle of cold water. For the last time, she looked over at Hushia. She wanted her to wake up. She went out and stood in the doorway and turned around. Then she hurried out and stood over the sleeping stranger's head like a phantom.

"Take this and eat."

Maadul the Upper Egyptian looked up in fright at the plate of food being offered to him. He was paralyzed for a moment. What was this? Who was this? Halima was surprised at his unease. She had thought he had stayed up to sing to her. She bent over him and spoke to reassure him.

"I'm Halima, sir."

Halima, the lady of this house, was beside him. It was after midnight and the whole village was asleep, even the dogs. He could not believe it. This was an accursed she-demon disguised as a woman. He was sure that if he put his hand out to the plate of food, whatever he touched would turn out to be a demon's mirage. He was a poor man. Why did the demons wish him ill? Under his breath, he rapidly recited the Verse of the Throne, but this was a powerful demon, for she did not vanish into thin air. She leaned over him and said, "Here, drink some water and don't worry." He moved away from her slightly. If he had been able to move his paralyzed feet, he would have run like the wind. He tried to get up, but she grasped his shoulder and leaned on him. He felt drugged and dizzy when he smelled her sweet southern perfume. Finally his voice prevailed over the paralysis of his shock.

"You're the lady of the house?" he asked, frightened.

"Who else should I be?"

That was her voice, for sure. He had heard it many times when she called him to have a meal or tea, or perhaps to get his attention for something he had to do when she could not find the contractor. What had brought her here? Was she a demon's spirit playing with him, or really the lady of the house? She must have lost her way and taken him for someone else.

"I am Maadul, ma'am."

"I'm Halima."

"Is there anything you need?"

"I was worried about you because of the scorpions and snakes."

"I'm used to them, ma'am."

"Come and sleep inside. It's safer."

Where? Inside the house? By Almighty God, this was a demon's spirit that sought his ruin. If it really was Halima, it would be impossible for her to say something like that because he had plied his trade in these villages for years, and the people here were exactly like the Upper Egyptians when it came to morals; if anything, they were more prim and modest here. In his dealings with them, he respected their traditions, and they trusted him, and no one wished him ill. He could not believe what was happening in front of him. He struck a match—if she were a demon, she would catch fire. She blew it out and scolded him, "No one can see us, stupid." This was a strange sort of demon, unaffected by fire or Koranic verses. Should he shout for help or hit her over the head with his club? But he had begun to weaken. This was the first time in his life he had been touched by a she-demon or a human woman who wanted him. He extended his hand cautiously and touched her, stroked her hair, and felt both her warmth and her madness. Let her be whichever, a demon or the lady of this house; either way, he would enjoy what he had heard of since boyhood and adolescence, and what was there to lose? If she were a demon, that would be fine. She would drag him deep inside the earth and he would eat every luscious thing, like meat and apples—no more wormy cheese, cheap millet bread, or smelly onions. No more backbreaking work. She would take him to meet the king of the demons. What was the difference between a demon and an angel, an Upper Egyptian or a southern one? There was no difference now. He walked behind her obediently, yearning for the magical world he would enter. She led him into the first room, where they kissed and hugged, in a stupendous moment that took them outside of time and place.

7

Hushia al-Nur had slept enough, and sat up in bed, wiping away the streams of sweat and drinking water. Her throat was dry after a terrifying dream in which she had seen phantoms climbing the walls and dropping into the courtyard. She had watched them enter her room and break into the box where she kept her valuables and her shroud. Ever since she had gone blind, her dreams were all about burglars and robberies; gangs from Upper Egypt had been invading the resettled Nubian villages. Her dream tonight had been a long one. "May God make it all well," she muttered. Shaya's daughter had rebelled against her. If it weren't for her, the girl would never have had a husband! And how many spinsters there were in this land! All infidel, ungrateful women. It was her fault: she had chosen Halima herself and would just have to wait until her son returned and brought her back into line. And she would tell her son to find a different wife.

"Halima."

She called out again, and then a third time, and listened anxiously, then approached Halima's bed and reached out to pinch her where it would hurt. The bed was empty. She called out, but no one answered. She groped around. No one. Was it really a dream that she had seen, or had thieves broken into the house and killed Halima? She listened carefully and cocked her head in all directions. With her fine hearing, she could hear even the faintest sounds, including birds, bats, and insects. And the whispers of conspirators. There was something suspicious, and she was trying to locate the source. A voice or voices, rough and graceful. She moved as quietly as a cat, as warily as a fox, with an elderly cunning. She knew every inch of the house; she had trained herself after many falls. Here, the floor swelled; here was a shallow hollow; behind her was the oven and the cattle pen; the water jug was to the left; the entrance was ten yards away; the stone wall was to the right. She leaned against the wall, letting it guide her to her target. At the doorway she found the source of the whispers and stopped so that her sandals made no sound. She stifled a scream of fear. She silently prayed. *There is no power or strength save in God.* She could not stand up. She was trembling, shocked. This could be nothing but the moaning of a whore. She almost fell, thunderstruck. This was a shameful thing she had never heard before. *What is going on here, Lord?* She moved in and flailed the air with her arms. She felt a rough leg, then two smooth legs, spread apart. She let out the scream she had been holding in, and it came out piercing and loud: "Help! Help! Help! Disgrace! Help me, people!"

In one bound, Maadul the Upper Egyptian was out of the room, and then out of the house, running as fast as he could, until he was swallowed by the darkness. Halima, now alert, thought only of silencing the shrieking old woman, of pleading with her, or stopping her mouth.

"Please, Hushia, protect me!"

Hushia was blind and deaf to her pleas, but her voice was deafening; it tore the silence to shreds. Unthinkingly, Halima moved her hand from Hushia's mouth to her throat, and with all her fear and hatred, she crushed it, and kept crushing it until all breath was extinguished. She only wanted to silence her, but was horrified at the sight of the strangled Hushia. She dressed quickly and went out to the threshold of the house to finish what Hushia had started. "Help! Help! Help me! The Upper Egyptian has killed Hushia al-Nur!" The sound echoed until the whole village was awake, and then women's voices sounded here and there, and then an army of women appeared in their long black wraps. They crowded around Halima, shouting and wailing. The men all set out behind Abbas Tawfiq with their clubs and lanterns, hunting the Upper Egyptian murderer. They fanned out over the farmland and looked in doorways, searched the abandoned houses and the hollows, and approached the drowsy villages of Upper Egypt; and the silent, desolate night of the land of Kanz was transformed into a grand funeral.